# Wainwright

by

Art Myers

This is a work of fiction. Any reference to historical events, real people, or real places are used fictitiously. Otherwise, characters, places, and events are products of the author's imagination.



Cover design by Janet L Blankenship

Contact Art Myers: artmyersbooks@gmail.com

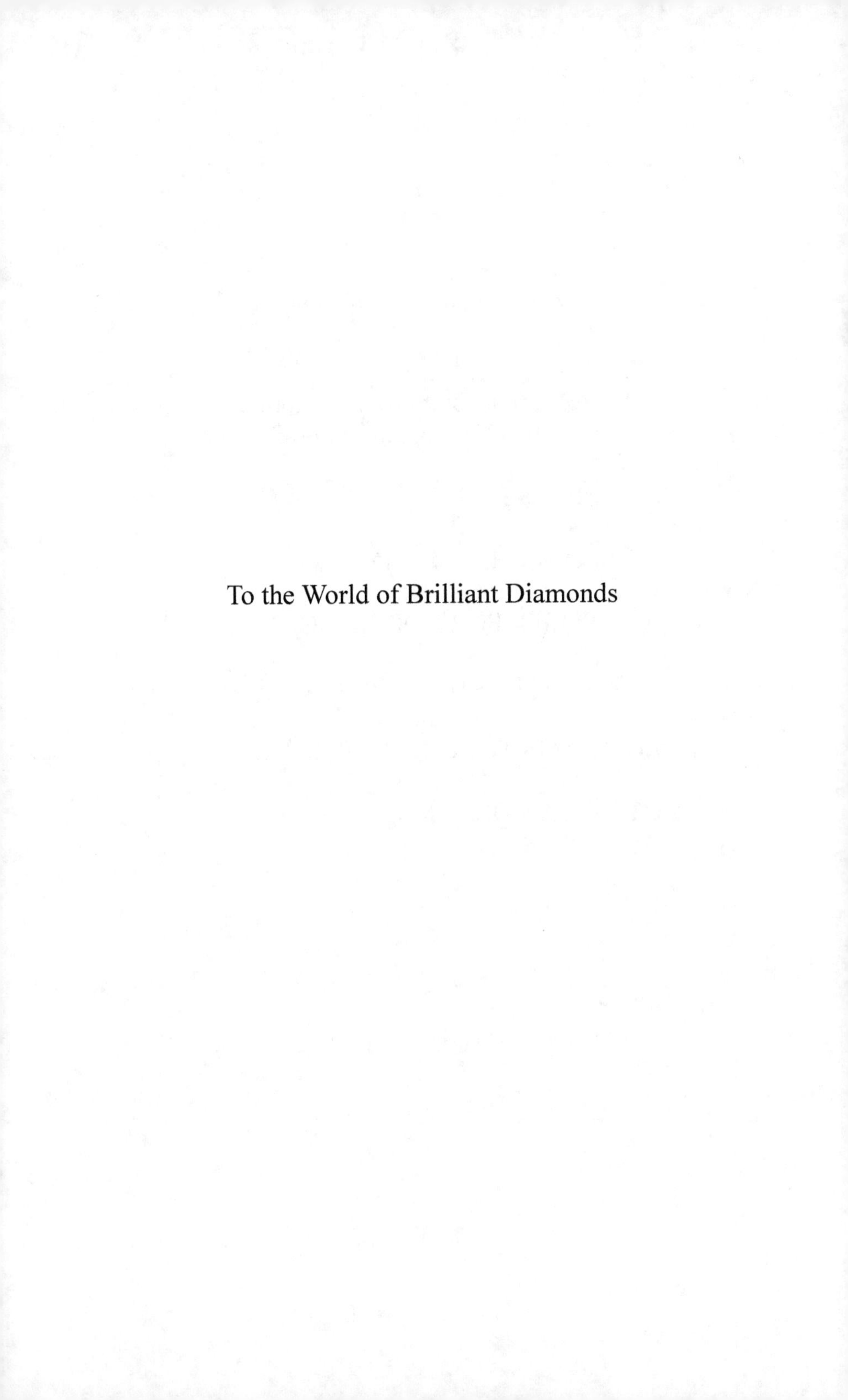

To the World of Brilliant Diamonds

Other Books by Art Myers

MY STORY
How A Young Boy From California
Ended Up An Old Man In Florida

ANDREW'S PIANO

ED ADAM CHASES A DREAM

A NEW LIFE FOR ROBERT JOHNSON

10,000 YEARS - Before Present

ED ADAMS TOUCHES THE STARS

CYNTHIA'S DREAMS

# Wainwright

# Chapter 1

Walter Wainwright walked toward his van in the Denver International Airport economy parking lot at 10:45 the morning of September 6, 2023. It had been an uneventful trip for a Wednesday early flight from Washington, D.C. and his planned drive home to his cabin, as he called it, should have him there before dark. He was tired, needing rest and recovery from the ten day operation he had just completed. It hadn't gone well and he was depressed at having made such an effort but losing the young man he had gone to rescue. It happens as the odds are always against one when trying this type of kidnapping rescue. Three men had died and it had almost been four, himself.

The Mercedes-Benz Sprinter Van was where he had parked it and a quick walk around showed no signs indicating it having been touched. It was a special modified version in both interior and drive. Speed of 150 mph was easily available. Full electronics, an additional fuel tank and comfort and amenities designed to make it home for months if necessary. The big engine started on the first turn, the dash screen showed all systems normal and he was soon handing the gate attendant his credit card. Touching the navigation icon and fastest route he had the command to turn right in fifty feet. He was on I-25 north bound in thirty minutes.

At Fort Collins a short detour had him on one of

his favorite highways, 287 North, and he was soon to the outskirts of Laramie, Wyoming joining Interstate 80 traveling west to Rawlins, then following 287 northward towards Lander. He expected to arrive there about 4:30 pm and would stop for a rest and dinner. It was a nice day for driving and the traffic was surprisingly light. He felt good, even with the aching muscles and the new flesh wound on his right side, just above his hip. He decided no more rescue attempts in warring nations would be taken in the near future. Too many things could go wrong, as they had this time.

He pulled into the parking area for The Hitching Rack surprised by the lack of any cars or trucks as the lot should have been half full by this time. He then remembered it was only open Thursday through Sunday. Not only was his biological clock screwed up, so was his calendar. He wanted to have their special hamburger with a draft beer and had been thinking about it for the last hour. Now he would have to settle for less if he was to make it home while it was still light.

Driving around the building he sighted a somewhat beat up white pick-up with a big man in the bed tossing out it's contents on the ground behind the restaurant. A large duffel bag had a Rossignol ski bag laying atop of it and a TaylorMade golf bag was off to the side. Two more soft sided suitcases and a big hanger bag followed in short order. The man was red faced and appeared to be cursing with each throw. A clothes bag hit the pile, then a banker box and then a second one which missed the pile, splitting apart on landing scattering books, folders and papers.

Walt couldn't decide whether to get involved with this spectacle or just watch it play out. His decision was made when the big man dragged a young woman out of the pick-up cab, yelling profanities and pushing her onto the pile. She made no effort to defend herself but held her head up staring at her assailant.

He seemed half crazed and Walt was sure he was on some kind of drug, or drunk. He continued his ranting and when he saw Walt approaching he turned his wrath on him. Walt was ready if he made a move on him and was not intimidated. He had handled situations like this many times before and the man sensed at the last minute it might be wiser to take his leave. With one last profane shout at the woman, sitting on the pile of what must be her worldly possessions, he got back into his truck and with a loud roar of the engine and spinning wheels throwing gravel on all behind them he made his exit. There was a blast of a horn and screeching of tires on the pavement by another vehicle on the highway, then a silence came over the scene.

Walter knelt in front of the young woman. Her gaze remained directly ahead and she did not acknowl-edge his presence. A flush on her right cheek foretold the possibility of swelling to come followed by a significant bruise. It was her eyes that Walt would remember the rest of his life. They were a blue gray, the color of a thin cloud backed  by a bright blue sky. The vacant look was familiar to him as she was in shock and semiconscious. She held a padded PC case tightly to her chest and wouldn't let him take it from her when he offered to help her stand up.

"My name is Walter Wainwright. I am your friend and will take care of you. Can you hear my voice?" he asked in an assuring manner as he lightly placed his hand on her bare arm.  She  nodded  her head so he continued,

"I am going to pick you up and carry you over to my van. I will place you on the bed inside. I want you to rest there as I put all your things in the van. After that is done we will sit and talk about what has just happened here. You have nothing to fear from me. Is this okay with you?" he asked in the same soft voice and she again nodded her head in agreement.

Walt carried her to the van and entered through the side door placing her on the queen size bed, covered her with a blanket and positioned her head on a pillow.

"I am going to start the engine and back the van to where your things are, load them into the van and will then be here with you. We can talk about what you want or need then. I am your friend."

He didn't wait for an answer and had everything loaded in fifteen minutes. He managed to collect all the papers, folders and books from the Bankers box that had split apart. He was surprised of the quality of her belongings. The best in the way of golf clubs, skis and luggage.

One last careful look around the site of the mayhem was made and a small length of a fine gold chain glittered in the dirt. He carefully pulled it up from the broken end and at the clasp was what looked to be a very small gold coin. The chain was complete, broken midway, and by luck the coin had slid to the intact clasp.

Entering the van he was surprised at seeing his new charge sitting up starring at an iPad screen. "Walter Wainwright of Dubois, Wyoming only shows an address and a telephone number available for sixty-five cents. Is that you? I don't want to waste that much on a wrong number?" was said with a smile that had Walt falling in love with this someone he knew nothing about and had been minutes ago a forlorn victim of some brutish thug.

He sat at the edge of the bed and took a long look at the young woman he had just saved from a situation most would have taken weeks to recover from. She was beautiful and also must be closer to thirty years old, not the young twenty something he had first thought. Her eyes were now clear and he couldn't look away from her gaze. Perfect teeth and an even smile that could bring one to whomever she shared hers with. Her hair was light brown, shoulder length and messed up in a nice way. The bruise was forming on her check and some tearing was caked with dust from the parking area. Walt reached to wipe it off with a finger tip and she didn't flinch from his touch.

"I don't think Walter, or Walt, will do as a name for my hero. I will find a new one for you when the time is right. What are you going to do with me now?" she asked with such good humor that Walter Wainwright was caught off guard.

They sat there for several minutes, just looking at each other, trying to read what was happening. "Suzanne Sussman," was announced by the beautiful woman now sitting up but still in Walter Wainwright's camper van bed. "Suz is just fine for me but what am I to call you? I guess Walt will have to do for now."

Walt handed her the gold chain with the small coin and her other hand went to her neck to search for it not being there. The flash of a frantic look came to her face and was immediately replaced by a look of joy. She reached for Walt and pulled him to her, kissing him on the lips. She did not pull away and Walt didn't want her to.

# Chapter 2

Suz relaxed her hold on Walt's arm and smiled as she saw the expression on his face. "I think Walt might not be such a bad name after all. We can work on that later if there is one. So what are you going to do with me?" was asked in such a way that it left him without an answer.

It was the laughter that came to both of them at that moment that would make their relationship so special. He finally came to his senses and suggested they head to Dubois, find a place to have some dinner and plan to stay in the Dubois Campground that night. She nodded her head in approval and kissed him a second time.

In a little over an hour they were entering the very small town and Walt drove directly to the campground. He pulled into one of the better slots and was greeted by the owner in such a personal way that Suz knew he had stayed there a number of times before. She was now wondering how far away from Dubois was his home, but didn't ask.

The answer came when Jack, the attendant, asked him if it being too late to get up to his cabin tonight. Walt responded he wouldn't try to drive the van up there in the dark. It wasn't that the van couldn't make the grade, it was if it got too close to the old mining road's edge.

Suz made use of the more than adequate bathroom in the van to freshen up and for the first time that day saw her face. It was what it was but she had no doubt that she was still an attractive woman in her early thirties. She couldn't suppress her smile at thinking how this day had turned out. From one of the worst days to one that had such promise. Walter Wainwright was probably the most interesting and attractive man she had ever met. She had met many before, even married to one but that seemed to be many years ago. She now had this person she was attracted to as if in a dream. "Don't you wake up, what ever you do!" was her thought as she toweled off her face and returned to see him intently entering information on his iPhone.

"Got time for me, good looking?" she asked and the phone was pocketed. He took her hand they started a walk to the Village Cafe passing by the National Bighorn Sheep Center.

"Tomorrow I will give you the tour of Dubois, Wyoming. This will be our first stop. The golf course will be next. Then the grocery store and maybe lunch here in the van," was Walt's response to this woman that had captivated him at the first look.

Ordering was easy. The hamburger plate with a draft beer for each with no hesitation on Suz's part in ordering the same as Walt. A walk along the river trail was a nice way to finish this part of their first day together. Evening had changed to night as they returned to the van. They both needed some time on-line and they sat in the swiveled captain chairs, side by side, pecking away at their keyboards.

Suz closed up her iPad first and looked at Walt as he concentrated on what he was doing. He was a handsome man. Several inches taller than her five foot ten, well built and already had proven to her to be strong and confident. She liked what she was seeing and even more important what she was feeling. It had been years since she had the desire for another man in her life. It hadn't been of importance to her since her husband had been killed in a car accident almost seven years ago. A cement truck had mistaken a confusing left hand turn light and turned in front of his small, and not seen, Porsche Speedster.

He had been a top salesman for John Deere Golf Course Equipment covering almost all of Northern California. They had a nice apartment in San Francisco and her fledgling business was just coming into it's own. One minute all was almost as good as life could provide and in the next it was gone. Six years had passed and although her business was successful she had not found the happiness she wanted.

One of her on-line associates had offered a room in Lander with her and her boyfriend if she wanted a change. San Francisco was on a downward spiral as far as safety and habitability was concerned and the cost of living had spiraled in the opposite direction. On a whim she had accepted the offer and it took only ten months to find her siting on the pile of her possessions behind The Hitching Rack restaurant. What a mistake it had been. Her friend had decided she had had enough of her bad choice and she left secretly in the middle of the night without so much as a goodbye. It had been after a solid month of arguments and physical abuse between them and was no surprise to Suz but he had then turned his anger onto her. She had told him were to go, standing her ground and felt lucky with no car at the time to be sitting on her stuff behind the restaurant. How lucky she had been was answered before she even had a chance to think of what she should do next.

Looking at Walt a faint smile crossed her face. He seemed to have finished what he had been working on and she slid her bare foot over onto his in a comfortable, teasing way. He looked at her and knew what was about to happen. He closed up his iPad, stood pulling her to him and the motions began. Turning off the lights up front they went back to the bedroom and undressed without embarrassment. Suz was the most beautiful woman he had ever been with and the only woman he had been attracted to in years. It was not rushed and they satisfied their desires together as if they had been lovers before.

The ritual was repeated once more before sleep came for both and then again in the morning when awakening. They exchanged smiles acknowledging with each other that it was meant to have happened and that they would be together for the next weeks, months, years and maybe the rest of their lives.

They had a late breakfast at the first open restaurant they came to and then the planned visit to the Big Horn Center. Walt had visited often and donated appropriately many times. Suz had a wonderful time as it is an excellent exhibit of one of the most prized animals of North America.

As they walked about town they held hands and purposely made contact with hips and shoulders, often stopping for a casual embrace. Neither thought it could be possible to be in love this way so quickly, but it had happened.

In the early afternoon, after another hour in the van, it was time for Walter to get back to his cabin high up in the hills northwest of Dubois. First he drove the short distance to Antelope Hills Golf Course and they walked about the clubhouse as Suz wanted to take a look at the practice area. The plan was to play as soon as Walt's injury heeled. A comment by Suz that he had managed other activities without seeming handicapped had her asking what his handicap at golf was. A ten was not bad and matched hers by less than two strokes. They would play even.

Soon after they left the highway the road became dirt and a dust trail was being left behind the big vehicle. Twenty minutes later, after several hundred yards of a precarious section of narrow road with a frightening drop off on the passenger side, they entered a meadow and wooded area at the head of which was a small log cabin built against the wall of the hillside. It was not the least impressive but what was inside was.

# Chapter 3

It was three steps up to the veranda style porch. The logs and floor planks were old and weather beaten. The door was the same but just slightly bigger than normal. A big, wrought iron handle and latch was topped by a big key slot and Walt centered his key and turned it a quarter turn clockwise. The sound of mechanical tumblers being moved into place was unexpected and the clunk that came next was loud enough to draw Suz's attention to what was happening at this most common looking old door.

Walt pressed the latch down and the six inch thick door opened automatically. He walked in, taking a quick look around and as the interior had been lit up, turned to Suz inviting her into his life. At least the current one. It was a big, square shaped  great room, the dimension of the entire front of the outside of the building but deeper by twice. A well furnished living space, big kitchen and dinning area. A wood fireplace with a large hearth. The floor was hardwood with large native American design rugs spaced where needed. The windows were to the front and on the side walls sides only half way to the back. From the inside they look to be normal glass windows but were actually one way glass with unnatural clarity. Large TV screens to the rear of the room showed views off to the sides of the cabin.

Suz stood perfectly still with a look of concern on her face. She was intelligent enough to realize that this was not just a cabin in the mountains. It was a fortress disguised as an old 1900s miner's cabin. She looked at Walt and  he could see the uncertainty in her eyes.

"Welcome to my world. Don't be alarmed at what you see here. It is what you think but that time for me is coming to an end. Having you in my life has me thinking the time is now," was said by Walt with such sincerity that she began to relax.

Suz took another look around and went over to the kitchen area. Nothing but the best was there. She opened the Sub-Zero refrigerator door and saw it fully stocked, the freezer likewise. In the corner a door opened automatically when she approached and the pantry there was also fully stocked. She didn't like what she was seeing and couldn't hide it from Walt.

"What kind of place is this. A bomb shelter? A fort to hold the last stand in? Jesus Walt, what are you involved in?" She asked the questions and visibly started shaking.

Walt took her hand and walked her to the middle of the back wall and again a door automatically opened, this time into a hallway. It was sided with several conventional doors and opening the first one on the right side showed a large and very well appointed master bedroom. There were large screen TV screens where one would expect windows. The views were of the countryside outside, beyond the hillside containing this portion of the house. At that moment several mule deer were grazing in a meadow that spread out to the horizon. An inside door showed the bathroom which was of like quality. Two large closets completed the master suite.

Walt guided Suz into the room opposite the master bedroom suite and her distress became even greater. It was the operations room for his rescue planning. A dozen TV screens were on the wall, three of which were showing at the time, unfortunately, the body camera records of his last rescue attempt. Suz recognized him on one of the screens just as the gun battle had started. It only lasted a minute but the sound was on and the shots and targets were easily identified. Even the shot that grazed Walt's side could be recognized by the jerk of his camera as the bullet hit him. The kills of the three kidnappers were visible and the retrieval of the lifeless kidnap victim was covered. The date code at the bottom of the screen was four days ago.

"I don't want to be here. You shouldn't have shown me any of this. You should have left me on that pile of my stuff in Lander." Her tears had started and Walt took her outside to the porch. They sat close together on the porch bench and watched the deer grazing as sunset approached. The beauty of the place began to calm Suz's nerves and she took Walt's hand in hers and asked, "Tell me about what it is you do. I need to know about it. All of it!"

# Chapter 4

"It was one of those things you don't realize what it is you are doing until it is too late. I was in ROTC at San Diego State University studying for a bachelor of science degree in engineering. Without thinking about what I was doing I ended up in a special operations training unit with the Marines at Camp Pendelton. It was a rescue unit that had ties to the FBI set up to retrieve marines that had been captured, or kidnapped, anywhere in the world. Ten years ago I was recruited by the FBI to work on rescuing American citizens caught up in international incidents. The room you just saw is my office, I work alone and recruit from a pool when I plan an operation. If anything goes wrong with the operation all connections to me are erased." Walt had said this slowly and then waited for Suz to comment.

"Is that bandage on your side covering a bullet hole?" was all she asked about. "Yes," was Walt's one word answer.

The silence seemed to grow louder. The deer were all looking directly at them on the porch as if they too were waiting for more.

Suz finally asked the question she needed to know the answer to, "Is this what you want to do with your life?"

Walt didn't hesitate answering, "I have been thinking I wanted out and my last operation convinced me it was time. Meeting you has made the choice for me to do it now. This has been my life the last ten years. It is now over. All I have to do is make the call and I am out. All I own is in my van. All I want now is who is here sitting next to me."

Suz could see that he meant what he was saying and that he was willing to give it all up to keep her with him. With out hesitating she asked,"Will you make that call? Now!"

He took out his cell phone and touched one of his contacts. The speaker phone feature was on and Suz could hear the three rings. A voice answered after the third ring saying only, "Go ahead, Wainwright."

Walt said, "I am out as of now!"

The voice replied, "You are out as of now! All your records have been erased. You no longer have any access to us or our property. Do you understand?"

Walter Wainwright answered, "Yes," and the line went dead.

They sat quietly for a few minutes, then Walt stood and went to the door. He placed his key in the slot and made the clockwise quarter turn. Nothing happened and he left the key in place.

"We should have taken some things from the re-frigerator. How do power bars and a coke sound for dinner tonight and breakfast in the morning?" was asked in a humorous manner.

"Perfect!" Suz responded along with a long kiss that promised him much more.

Walt took out his iPhone and entered his Chase Bank Account. The minimum fee for his service of fifty thousand dollars had been deposited and if he had been successful in the rescue it would have been four times that. He had a good investment account, an IRA and was comfortable not having any income potential for the time being. He had not thought about what other things he might do after his high pressure rescue operations came to an end but he now had the time to find them.

For some odd reason he remembered a fishing trip north of Big Sky, Montana he had taken a few months ago and that a can of Dinty Moore Stew had been stowed in the locker with his fishing gear. Excusing himself for a moment he headed for the van and minutes latter proudly displayed to Suz his catch.

She jumped up, smiling at the sight of this man providing her such a treasure. It was dark when the stew was divided as they sat at the fold down table in the van. They were at home, together, and that night would be as was the night before.

Just before it was time for sleep, Walt asked Suz what she did to make her living and was greeted with her laughter.

"I have a search for missing children service I run mostly online with several associates. Might be something right up your alley handling the more difficult cases with abduction and kidnapping. Interested?"

That could wait until later as they were at that moment searching for other things they could do together to make life that much better for them both.

# Chapter 5

Walt turned into the campground and parked the van in the same slot he had parked it in the day before. Almost before he shut the engine off Jack was grinning up at him on the drivers side window.

"Weren't you just here yesterday? Can't keep away from the magic of the Dubois Campground?" was his friendly greeting. For some reason it gave Walt a good feeling. Almost like family welcoming him home after a long absence.

"We will be here a few weeks, at least for now. My cabin in the hills is no longer mine to use and that is a long story I won't talk about." Walt said this and hoped he could leave it at that. Dubois was a very small town and all living here knew most of what each other were doing. That could be a good thing, but not always. Just then Suz leaned over Walt enough to make eye contact with Jack and told him she was here too and he would never see Walt wandering around town alone again.

It was a good start for Walter Wainwright's new life as an unemployed spook and he was feeling much the better for it. Jack offered to hook up the van to power, water and sewer but Walt asked him to wait as they may have to make a few trips out today and tomorrow. The first was walking to the Village Cafe for breakfast and it was then across the highway to Lynn's Super Foods grocery store.

Thirty minutes later Walt and Suz realized they needed a car. Hooking up, and unhooking, the van to the utilities was inconvenient and they were planning to do some recreation that made using the big van a problem.

Once back to the campground and stowing their supplies Suz said she wanted to take another look at the Wind River that was just a hundred yards away. They found a bench and sat together watching the water flowing by. Fall was here but this year the volume seemed good and watching the rivulets, swirls and currents was mesmerizing.

Suz grabbed Walt's arm and excitably exclaimed, "Did you see that!" pointing in the direction of some flat water. There was another telltale sign of a trout rising to take a fly and Walt did see it.

"Can we fish here. Right in the middle of town?" was asked with an excitement in her voice that pleased him. He was a good fly fisherman and answered that he thought so but did she have a fly rod and a Wyoming license.

"Let's get my ski bag out and see what is in it besides my skis." There was an aluminum rod case containing a fine graphite fly rod and in the big duffel was a loaded fishing vest and hip waders. Soon they were exhibiting their casting by laying their fly on targets set about in the park.

Walt was pleased to see how skillful she was and realized Suz could probably match him in most things in life. It was a good realization and he was wondering if all this was too good to be true.

Jack had come out to see the competition in the yard and he let on he knew some good spots upstream he would point out to them. The three ending up sitting on a near by picnic bench and passing the end of the day talking about things of little importance such that each could judge the character of the other. It was soon obvious that Jack was more than a campground supervisor. He was well read and a good conversationalist.

Walt made the suggestion that he and Suz would need a car to run the every day errands and short trips to play golf and go fishing. Jack knew someone that had what they might find of interest. Mary White, a ninety-six year old widow living here most of her adult life, had a 1980s Jeep Wagoneer. It was like new and she needed a bit more income to live out her last years. Besides, she hadn't been able to drive for over ten years.

That evening Walt and Suz were busy on their iPad's after having their first home cooked meal together. Suz had a project going and Walt was researching Waggoneers.

"Want to drive to the golf course in a twenty-five thousand dollar, forty year old jeep?" Walt asked with a bit of sarcasm in his voice.

Suz looked up from her work and gave him a smile he was becoming used to and liked. "It depends on how much you want to help an elderly lady in her last few years. You can help her sell it to a collector and buy what we need. I would think that the better approach."

"Point well taken. I will suggest we set it up that way if we get that far. You about finished with what you're doing and have a few minutes for me?" was asked and answered in an most enjoyable way. Walt thought he was in heaven if such a place existed. He was sure about there being a place as hell as his last few years had been there.

# Chapter 6

Jack was leading the way to their visit with Mary White who lived only a few blocks from the Campground. It was a nice morning, the air felt crisp and light jackets were zipped up. He knocked on the door and it was immediately opened by a young woman. They were welcomed in to meet the most interesting and delightful Mary White.

It was a small house sitting on a small lot with no landscaping. Just the brown earth but it was clean in it's own way. Neat, came to Walt's mind. The driveway to the single detached garage was gravel and was again clean and was nicely bordered by small rocks. The house was entered from a centered front door directly into the living room area which also included the dining room. The kitchen was visible through the opening behind the dining room table and opposite that side was an open hallway that led to the two bedrooms and the single bathroom. Again, neat, clean and welcoming.

Mary looked to be a small woman in her big chair, with dark brown eyes that were dancing with the excitement at having guests. In her mid-nineties she had outlived all her friends and acquaintances here in Dubois and had few others to entertain. It took only minutes for the four of them to have a robust conversation underway.

As they talked Suz's eyes kept drifting toward the collage of black and white framed photographs mounted on the wall behind Mary. She noticed and asked Suz to go take a closer look and see if she recognized anyone.

"That's Charlie Chaplin and I am guessing the couple next to him are your mother and father. Am I right about that, Mary? That's Roscoe "Fatty" Arbuckle and Max Sennett.  Mabel Normand is there with your mother and father. Tell us about it. Is the baby Mabel is holding in this one you?"

"Oh my dear girl, you're so much smarter than anyone I have ever known. Why would you know all of this? About these people? You are right on all counts. Sit here by me, and I will tell you about what you are looking at." Mary had found a soulmate and suggested the boys go out to the garage and take look at the Wagoneer.

She started by telling Suz that the photographs were from her mother's collection of her, and her father's, time working for Mabel Normand. These were her favorites and had always been displayed somewhere in their home. They had left the booming Hollywood life shortly after she had been born in February,1927 and moved first to Lander and then here to Dubois when she had entered school.

"My father was in love with Mabel, as was every man that met her, when he first met my mother. He had been in the early movie business as a handy man. They call them a grip now days when they take care of all the camera and lighting equipment. My mother was hired as an assistant and part time secretary for Mabel and they became close friends. To her last days, whenever Mabel Normand was mentioned, she would say what a fine person she was and so talented, both as an actress and as a director. Mabel died young, at thirty-six, from tuberculous. I was only three years old then and didn't realize how much it had hurt my mother." Mary went on to tell a few of the stories her mother had told her of her time with Mabel. How she and her father had fallen in love some time after it became obvious Mabel would only be a friend to him and they found that they should be together.

Walt and Jack headed for the small garage and with the key Jack unlocked the big padlock. "I haven't seen this car since Joe died, at least eight years ago. He hadn't driven it for five years before that. Almost afraid to see what it looks like," saying this last as he opened the bi-fold doors.

It was what was expected. Covered in years of accumulated dust with all four tires flat. The big white wall tire casings were cracked from age and the rubber discolored. Despite this, the 1983 Wagoneer Limited's special red paint was trying to shine through the dirt, the side paneling the correct colors and the chrome looked unblemished.

Jack gave the keys to Walt and offered the honors to him. With a towel he had brought with him Walt carefully dusted the area around the drivers side door, inserted the key into the door lock and twisted it in the correct direction. A familiar click and the lock stem popped up.

Smiles broadened on both of their faces and Walt pressed the button on the door handle and opened the door. The inside sparkled in a special way, the smell was neutral and the leather upholstery look like new. Any doubts about the outside were replaced with a new confidence.

The hood was dusted off to open it after the latch handle was pulled. It had popped up just enough to reach the inside latch and Walt nodded to Jack to do the honors. The big V-8 was dust covered but look remarkably good. The radiator was sound, hoses old but in place, ignition wires likewise. Even the battery terminals were clean although the battery was dead, and had been for years.

The two went to either side and lay down in the dust and dirt and saw the same thing. No signs of leaks and better than that, no signs of rat or mouse nests. The exhaust system was intact and solid.

Walt dusted himself off and took a seat on the driver's side. The odometer showed 17,756 miles. The dials and glass were clear and everything was in its place and could be expected to work. They had a gem on their hands and could make a good report to Mary. It would not be what Walt would want for a car as it was too valuable as a collector's automobile. He and Jack had a project to get Mary a good price for her Wagoneer.

While the boys were in the garage Mary had Suz come sit close to her and in a conspiratorial whisper she asked how long she and Walt had been together, Suz's answer of three days brought forth genuine laughter from Mary and she said, "I thought it had just happened," and added, "Does he treat you nice? Does he tell you he loves you?" She asked this with such excitement Suz knew at that moment she had a grandmother to talk to for the time that was left for this remarkable woman. Walt would soon come to have this same revelation.

# Chapter 7

As they walked back toward the Campground the three came to realized that a team was forming. Walt was the first to comprehend how much his life had changed in just the past three days. He was out from under a high pressure, high risk and lonely life into a love for a woman he could only have imagined in his dreams and also now had a new sense of freedom he had never known before.

Suz was wondering at what had just made her life so worth living again, with an optimism she had never experienced before. She had found a man she felt she had been waiting for and thought that true happiness may be achievable for her again. Every minute was now valuable and not to be wasted. Looking at Walt sent a thrill through her that he would be part of her life from now on.

Jack could only smile. He now had two friends, two more than he had ever had before. He liked the way Walt did things with such ease and how he accepted his input as valuable. He was sure the Wagoneer project was going to be just the beginning. For the first time in years he had something more than just managing a campground to look forward to.

Walt looked at Jack and asked him what he had been doing on his iPhone as they were examining the tires.

"I was texting a friend here in town to see if he could find exact replacements, and if he could order five of them. Might as well have the spare match the four on the ground. He will also be the man we need to get the car rolling. Bill Holden can take this beauty apart and put her back together in like new condition while we watch and agree to everything he suggests. All you have to do is pay his invoices, and you will be surprised how fair they will be." Jack said this speaking quickly not wanting anything to delay the project.

Mary agreed to the proposed twenty percent commission to be shared between the three of them, after the expenses, upon the sale of the Wagoneer. Walt had suggested it would bring a good price and with Jack and Suz's approval had suggested the twenty percent figure. Walt also told Jack he would get ten percent and he and Suz would split the other ten.

Suz wanted to walk back along the river trail so they detoured in that direction, found one of the many benches with a good view and sat together staring at the river. She was intently watching the water and both Walt and Jack were watching her. She was a beautiful woman and her intense gaze was understood by both the men when she pointed out a trout rising for a insect in a clear bit of water just downstream of a small boulder.

"Jack, can you fish here in town. I bet you I could catch that one on my first cast!" she said in a way that the only answer from the boys was how much should the bet be.

Ten minutes later Suz was back with her fishing gear and the bet was made. If she caught her trout the boys had to do the dishes after dinner that night. There was a bit of good-natured kidding as Suz slipped on her waders, set up her rod and reel and headed into the water's edge.

Jack was delighted. He had just been invited to dinner and would gladly do the dishes. Walt was bemused as he always did the dishes, or certainly planned to, whenever Suz cooked. They watched her as she selected a fly and tied on the leader tip. Next she took her pliers and flattened the barb of the hook, of which Walt and Jack both took notice. A few confident steps into the water had her in position, the line out and was setting up the distance with several back casts.

It all happened so fast that Walt and Jack could only admire the skill being shown to them by this beautiful woman who obviously knew what she was doing. Two more back cast and she let out the measured portion of he line she held as the line shot out straight and true, the small fly landing exactly where it was needed. The strike was immediate and Suz played the fish just long enough to demonstrate the catch, then slacked off the line to let the barb less hook release it's hold on the trout.

Jack, with a grin so big he could hardly speak, asked Walt, "Wash, or dry?"

Suz cast to several other prime spots and soon had another fish putting up an aerial demonstration. Several other people had been walking along the river trail and stopped to watch this attractive lady put on a show that would be remembered by them for years to come. Especially by the two that waited as she exited the river and came up to them with the smile they both now cherished.

# Chapter 8

It was their fourth morning and the start of their fifth day together. The love making was comfortable and not hurried. As they lay together both Walt and Suz were having the same thoughts and their laughter about what was going on had them both smiling.

"Well, big boy, will you kindly tell me what is happening between the two of us?" were her first words to him that morning.

"I'm not sure, but whatever it is I don't want it to change in any way. At this moment my life cannot be any better. You are with me and that is all I can ask for. I think we have a new friendship growing with Jack. I don't remember ever having a real friendship like this before. Then there is Mary White who has also brought some very special meaning into our lives. I wonder what will be next. Are you ready for it?"

There was a knock on the van's door and Suz said with more laughter in her voice, "Why don't you go find out what it is!" As she said this she pulled the sheet away and there was a question on Walt's face of what to do at that moment but Suz gave him the look that told him she would wait for him to come back after he learned what it was to happen for them next.

Jack was looking up at him with a good morning and sorry to interrupt your morning grin. He asked if he and Suz would like to visit one of those special fishing spots this afternoon and to plan on an evening cook out on the site with a most interesting character that they needed to meet. Walt had his answer to Suz's question, accepted the invitation and without delay was slipping back under the sheet to tell her about their next adventure. She answered without saying yes but in a way of showing enthusiasm that he could appreciate. That afternoon would be perfect to find out what adventure awaited but for the moment other things might better be continued.

The morning had been well spent and was followed with waffles for breakfast, in the van, just before noon. A long walk up river to the edge of town and back determined that right where they were located now was as good a place to be as anywhere else in town.

At two o'clock Jack arrived in his old jeep and they loaded their fishing gear and themselves into the cramped vehicle. Suz got the passenger seat and Walt sat on the bench seat among the gear in the back. No seat belts but in a few hundred yards they were off the paved highway, across the bridge toward the airport and then onto a patch-work of dirt roads headed northward along the river. A mile had them on almost trail like paths and they came to a gate sided on either side by short sections of fence. The gate seemed of no significance but Jack produced a key for the lock and re-locked it after they had passed through. Another mile had them parked under a large tree next to an old picnic table. There was a fire pit and a supply of fire wood. The Wind River was a short walk below and stretched in either direction with what looked liked excellent trout water.

They had hardly looked about the area when an

even older jeep than Jack's came into view and a grizzled old man jumped out to greet Jack and be introduced to Walt and Suz.

"Mary said you were nice kids and I trust her. Jack told me Suz could out fish anyone on this river, or in this state. Good! I have something for each of you."

Jack interrupted the old man with the introduction of Oliver Bennett, Ollie for short. Somewhat over ninety and owner of this little piece of property. He was about five foot seven and could weigh no more than 125 pounds. His grip was strong and his skin was wrinkled and looked like old leather.

"You first Suz," and he handed her a small plastic vial with two fishing flies inside. Next he gave a similar one to Walt. "Okay, here's the deal. I have just given you each two Renegade flies I tied this morning. They are weighted nymphs and with the small split shot sinkers pinched on your leader about two feet up will catch our evening meal. I want four 14 to 16 inch rainbows. No smaller or bigger. No brown trout. Only rainbows. Jack and I will prepare the German fried potatoes. It is three and cocktail hour starts at four-thirty, so get busy. Jack can go fish with you for a bit and I am going to sit over there on that rock and watch the best fisherman in Wyoming catch my dinner."

The three prepared their rods and Walt and Suz tied on the flies with the small split shot placed as instructed. When they reached the river's edge Jack gave a few words of advice. "Ollie means what he says on the size of the trout and he is serious about the time. I will fish for a short while then go help with the picnic. Also, you might not realize that there are always a number of nice trout in the first ten feet from shore. No sense wading out to start fishing for what may be swimming about your feet. Then work you way farther out. You don't have to go past midstream to catch our supper and as soon as you have that done spend a little time to hook a few really big brown trout."

Ollie had taken his seat on the big boulder. What handsome young people he was watching, and he thought how old he had gotten. His parents had come west from Chicago as newlyweds in 1920 to start a small bakery and restaurant in Lander. The Chicago and North Western Railway had led to a boom as it reached Lander toward the end of 1906 but the plans to extend rail service on to Oregon or California had been scuttled and Lander became known as where the rails end and the trails began. They moved to Dubois, starting a second bakery restaurant, and this was where Ollie had been born in the Spring of 1930. He was their only child.

Mary White's parents had moved to Dubois from Southern California that year with their three year old daughter. It was never clear to Ollie what they did to make a living but he thought it had something to do with the motion picture industry. It was Mary that had become his best friend and the only girl he had ever loved. When his growth had stopped and she continued to a tall five foot eight, gone away to college and came home after graduating engaged it had left him the love sick bachelor he still was.

The fishermen quickly met the requirements set for them and then for the next half hour had some of the best trout fishing they had ever experienced. Suz topped the catch with three browns, the largest was estimated to be twenty-eight inches.

The cocktail hour was spent on Ollie's boulder with plastic wine glassed filled from a bottle with no label. It was chilled white wine and was incredibly good. A second bottle was opened as Ollie and Jack prepared the meal. Suz and Walt watched as the fires were stoked into a healthy bed of coals, the big cast iron skillets were placed directly on the coals. A cup of Crisco was melted in the bigger skillet and the sliced onions and potatoes added, stirred occasionally and seasoned with salt and pepper. In the smaller skillet the trout were cooked in some kind of seasoned oil that Ollie had brought.

It seemed to be an odd combination to both Suz and Walt until they had their first few bites of each. All grew quiet as the four cemented a new friendship over one of the finest meals the two newest members had ever experienced.

# Chapter 9

As twilight approached, and after a third bottle of unlabeled wine was emptied, the site was cleaned up, the coals quenched by several buckets of water and the fishing equipment stowed in Jack's jeep. Ollie was offered a thank you with a handshake from Walt and a much appreciated hug and kiss on his cheek by Suz.

On the ride back to the campground Jack offered a little more on Ollie's background. That he had lived almost his entire life here in Dubois and still lived in the house he had been born in. Jack would see if they could visit him there as it would be quite a surprise and nothing like what they might expect. Ollie had spent time in the service in the first years leading up to the Vietnam fiasco and was able to be in other areas as it began to heat up in earnest. He left the service with a very small benefit and supplemented this income by being able to fix anything that needed fixing and tying flies in demand beyond his desire to tie them. His wants were few and his expenses less. He was a good man and Jack considered him his only living relative even though they were not actually related.

Nestled in bed that night Walt and Suz forsake any intimacies and just enjoyed what this day had afforded them. How good it was to meet such interesting people in such a small, out of the way place. There was something of a mystery to it all as in just these past few days they had met two extraordinary, elderly people they wished to be more acquainted with.

Suz then started the conversation about how she had recognized the people in the photographs on the wall at Mary White's house. That as an assignment in one of her college courses was to write a research paper on a person of note from a list recommended by the instructor. She had picked Charlie Chaplin as she liked old movies, especially the short ones of the silent film genre. In doing the research she became even more interested in Mabel Normand and did a second paper on her.

"There is some, subtle connection between Mary and Mabel other than her parents. I have no idea what it could be but I can sense it." Suz said this with such determination that Walt had no doubt he would be involved in at least a part of the research. Research was an important part of what he had done and not only was important for the information gained but his life had depended on it.

"I think we can work on this together. I don't have direct access to the research facilities I once had but I know those who do. Many of them had depended on my work to get them through some of the tough assignments they were given. We have another of interest that I am sure has a story worth knowing in Ollie. His past is not that of the small town lad he and Jack would have us believe. A partnership?" he asked and Suz helped that partnership along with an answer without words.

Monday morning was very similar to the morning before and at about the same time there was a knock on the van's door. Again it was Jack with the same apologies and the word that his friend Bill Holden would meet them at Mary White's to put the Wagoneer up on jack stands and take the wheels, including the spare, to his shop to prep them for the new tires that would be arriving Monday afternoon from Denver. As things often go the preparation of the Wagoneer to sell went quickly. By Tuesday afternoon it would be in his shop and they could drain all the fluids, flush what was necessary and re-fill with the best available replacement. The gas tank and fuel lines were drained and flushed as was the carburetor. A new battery installed along with spark plugs and ignition parts. It was then time to start the engine and see if the jeep would move, and also stop.

It did and with some very minor adjustments the big engine purred as if brand new, the exhaust system was sound, the automatic transmission worked beautifully, as did the brakes. The ride was smooth and it was time for the cosmetic team to do their tasks. Photographs were taken by Suz and an online sales brochure was laid out. A few minor corrections on the specifications were made and then had them ready to set up the marketing parameters. A best offer in thirty days was going to be offered with a minimum starting bid of $25,000 established.

What happened next was a surprise. The bidding went immediately to $57,000 and then stopped. It would turn out that on the last day for bidding one last challenge to the $57,000 was made but the counter of $60,500 was the winning bid. A week later the 1983 Jeep Wagoneer Limited was on a trailer headed for Tulsa, Oklahoma with the new owner satisfied with the addition to his collection.

This was all in the future and much was to happen as the preparation and sale of Mary's husband's pride and joy found a new home and Mary had a nice addition to her savings to carry her through her remaining years.

# Chapter 10

Bill Holden found a 2015 Jeep Wrangler that fit Walt's eye and pocket book. A check and trip to the Motor Vehicle Department had the paperwork done and the new plates on the jeep. Suz thought it good enough for the time being and as the adventures it took them on began to unfold it became a favorite.

Their first outing was a drive and camp out above the facility that Walt was at until he opted out just a week ago. It was also their first week anniversary. The idea of all that had happened for them in just one week together brought smiles to them both when Suz had commented about it as they drove pass the gate that guarded Walt's past.

Five more miles brought them to the camp site Walt had wanted to show Suz. Above timberline the peaks of the range to the East had just begun to take on the colors of a sunset. They had prepared to spend the night there and pitched the small tent, spread the double foam pad and placed the sheets and two blankets on the pad. A short hike of about a mile saw evening arrive and they enjoyed a simple dinner.

As they spread out the bedding and readied for what was known to be next Suz asked the question that Walt knew was coming, "Is this going to be enough?"

"No, it won't be. Fishing, golf, mountain climbing

and even making love will not replace the type of intellectual challenges we both need. We have one we can work on. You know what it might be and I want to go there with you. Mary could be Mabel Normand's daughter, but for some reason I don't think so. Everything is tied up around the end of 1926 and Mary's birth date but there is nothing in the records that comes close to telling us what it is."

Suz looked at Walt with such intensity that he was worried he had said this wrong. She then reached for him, pulling him close and saying, "I knew you saw it the minute I told Mary that I recognized the people in her photo collection. She knows and whatever it is that happened it has to be kept as her secret. It is Mabel's history that must be protected but I want to find out how Mary White was being held by Mabel Normand as a baby. Want to go on a little history hunt with me?"

Walt responded, "I have already started. Probably will catch up with you with another few hours on-line but so far the public record doesn't even suggest what might have happened. We do know that Mary's mother and father were both there at the time, married and had no children of their own. Let's work on this for as long as the trail is viable and maybe along that trail we can find another, more interesting and worth while search that we can follow."

They lay together, the silence so complete one could imagine being in another world. A world not as torn apart as was the one they were now part of. What had happened to all the good movement toward a better place that had seemed once again to be possible such a short time ago.

Walt started to hum the old Kingston Trio song

The Merry Minuet and Suz sang a favorite verse, "Italians hate Yugoslavs, South Africans hate the Dutch, And I don't like, Anybody very much."

"Let me show you how much I like you, my song bird," was Walt's answer and in turn Suz showed him how much she liked him.

It was the next morning as Walt was preparing pancakes, bacon and coffee on the old two burner camp stove that another event in their new lives together was to be revealed.

The first indication was the low rumble of a big engine driving what must be a four wheel drive vehicle up the steep grade below them. It would bring this new adventure into their lives in the next half hour. There was no where else it could go.

The early sunlight had just reached them and the mountain peaks to the west were now in broad daylight. Walt was plating the pancakes and bacon and they still had time to enjoy the breakfast before whoever was coming up the primitive road would reach their campsite.

As they put away their breakfast gear Walt had placed his small day pack next to him and slid his hand into it. The click, and then a second similar sound broke the silence and a scared look came to Suz's face. She was familiar with that sound, the release of the safety and the cocking of a handgun's hammer. He didn't take the gun out but it was now readied and within his reach. Suz had no idea why it would have been there and that was what was frightening her.

# Chapter 11

The big Jeep came into view as Walt and Suz were stowing the last of camp and cooking gear in the back of the Wrangler. Walt stood next it with his hand lightly resting on the day pack. Suz was two steps away and slightly behind him.

It came up the track and stopped about fifty feet away, the enclosed cab's door opened and a tall, well built man stepped out and waved a greeting to them. He was dressed in blue jeans, T-shirt covered by a down vest. His hands were bare, a ball cap was on his head and canvas shoes were on his feet. He was not dressed for hiking, or combat, was Walt's immediate thought.

Larry Nichols approached, introduced himself and offered that he was Walt's replacement at the site he had just left. He saw them drive by yesterday and took the chance to drive part way up the mountain and introduce himself if he found them.

He was younger than Walt by about ten years, handsome and in remarkably good shape. Walt knew he would have no chance against him in physical combat but decided there was no danger, at least not at this moment.

The introduction to Suz was a bit more tense as she was appraising Larry with some suspicion since Walt had indicated possible danger in the handling of his gun. They would discuss this later but she was confident that he was not going to pose any problem for her with Walt present. She was also immediately sure that he was gay and she was seldom wrong when making such a judgment.

The invite for dinner that evening at the cabin was accepted and the gate would be opened upon their arrival. Some additional small talk was made and then Larry took his leave.

"So mister Wainwright, what have they planned to get you back into their web. There has to be some connection with our on-line searching on Mabel Normand with why they want you back. At the moment I am just with you and I don't think that is, at least for now, important to them. I think our mister Nichols maybe gay but that is not relevant, either. Tell me your thoughts." Suz had asked this in a way that Walt knew demanded his answer.

He took her hands and drew her close. "This has no bearing on what I did with them in he past. I would never be asked to enter that world again. Once you have decided you have had enough it is to dangerous to place you back into a position where you have to make a quick decision on what to do when it is required. There are no second chances when dealing with the kind of people they need you to deal with. I agree this may have something to do with Mabel Normand. Her lovers, friends or even Mary White and her parents. Something long ago that has great value for one of their customers. Let's take our hike and then have a dinner that may have a surprise for dessert."

They stood together, as close as was possible, and Walt realized at that moment that he was in love with this interesting woman. There was no doubt in his mind anymore but it was her decision as to how it would turn out between them. He needn't have had any doubts as knowing came a short time later that day.

Their ascent of the unnamed peak was a gentle walk-up. Mostly a smooth hillside that could be walked side by side. Their stride was almost identical and they held hands most of the way. The last several hundred yards more closely resembled a peak and the rocky terrain required a little more care but was still an easy climb. A big boulder at the top provided a perfect seat giving them a 360 degree view of what was around them. They sat close together positioned with the best view of the most spectacular of the big mountain peaks that now seemed to be close enough to touch.

The temperature was near perfect, with only a slight breeze, and the quiet seemed surreal. Suz took Walt's hand and looking into his eyes said in a whisper, "I am in love with you, Walter Wainwright. Don't you break my heart."

# Chapter 12

The gate opened as they approached and Walt drove up to the front of the small cabin that hid what it contained. It had been only one week since he and Suz were sitting on the porch and he made the decision to leave what had been the reason to having been there. The chance meeting of Suz behind The Hitching Rack in Lander had changed his life in a way he had never thought possible. He felt no doubt of the choice he had made then and had no remorse as they approached the cabin now.

Larry greeted them, standing on the porch, in a friendly manner and they were invited inside with no hesitation. Drinks were offered and the cold beers were provided. He had the dinner menu laid out on the kitchen counter and the three rib-eye steaks were soon on the cook top grill. Baked potatoes were in the warming box and the salad prepared and chilled in the refrigerator. Twenty minutes was all it took to have the meal presented and the three enjoying it along with a friendly conversation. Ice cream and fresh baked cookies were served as the dessert.

They sat facing each other across the table and the look on Larry's face told both Walt and Suz it was now when he would tell them why they were here. Suz didn't wait and with the smile Walt was beginning to understand she asked the obvious question, "Larry, why don't you tell us why we are here. None of this was coincidence, so just spell it out for Walt and me!"

Larry's smile broadened and he said only, "Prince Mohammed Ali Ibrahim." There was a pause that lasted almost a full minute.

"How can you know I was searching that name. I first typed it in a on-line search yesterday. I just found it mentioned in the search of Mabel Normand I started three days ago. What is going on here?" Suz asked this although her fear was being replaced with a curiosity she couldn't hide. She realized that Walt already knew as he had shown no surprise at hearing the name. He had been making similar searches and he was sure his old employer would be monitoring his on-line use. He was surprised, however, at the connection with Mabel Normand would have their interest and he waited for Larry to explain. He reached for Suz's hand and she understood his signal, turned her gaze back to Larry and gave him a look that indicated it was his turn to answer her questions.

Larry Nichols was enjoying the moment so he looked at Suz and started with, "You should understand something about the man you are sitting next to. In this business a talent is required that few men, or women, have in making the right decisions and accomplishing their task when confronted by not only difficult choices but in many cases in extremely dangerous ones. Walt Wainwright was one of the best our organization has ever employed. Possibly the best. Ten years and twenty-eight of thirty successful operations."

Another pause, this one shorter, with a look toward Suz that indicated she would like what is coming, Larry continued, "Suz, it has come to our attention reviewing your work of the past few years that another opportunity for us to follow might be profitable, and much safer to perform, with still a very nice profit to be made. Your model for finding lost children and young people showed a technique that could be developed to find other valuable things, such as fine art and jewelry. Your search protocol is very efficient and has proven results. Walt's planning and retrieval is the best and the two of you working together would make a great team for our purpose."

Suz looked at Walt and he answered with a look that told her to wait. That Larry had set all this up and would explain it to them in his own way.

He offered refills of coffee which were accepted and the minor fuss of fixing and serving allowed the tension that had built up to dissipate. He then continued his presentation.

"A lot was happening in the world as the 1920s got underway. World War I came to a close, the Russian revolution had ended as did the one in Egypt. The powerful were shifting their positions and those that had been oppressed were about to be oppressed by those taking over from those just deposed. All was thus ending as it usually does. In Egypt the new king was King Fuad and one of his relatives was our Prince Ibrahim. As Fuad had said, he didn't show much, if any, interest in Egyptian politics. In his early twenties his interests were more in champagne, roulette, and beautiful women. Your Mabel Normand was one of those beautiful women. His world tour found him in Los Angeles in the spring of 1922 with more money available to spend than he could spend. They were together most of March of that year. She would say at the time she was just his friend but by his accounts he wanted to marry her. In mid June of that year Mabel had headed for

Paris and by more than just coincidence our Prince Ibrahim was also there. They were seen together at many of the important Paris social events but towards the end of this time they went their separate ways. They were still friends but the Prince was then courting another one of the lovely American actresses."

A longer pause came but the story was so well told that both Suz and Walt were satisfied to wait.

"So what is the purpose of me telling you all this that you both already know. Simply put, our Prince gave his lady friends many things. Some kept them, some sold them or gave them away. Mabel did all three. Among the jewelry pieces the Prince gave her was a very valuable necklace that was not actually his to give away. The ornate Tiffany presentation box was found in place but the necklace was missing and no one seems to have any idea where it was. It is still missing and there is a reward for it's return that far exceeds it's value as jewelry. Our client will gladly pay the possessor, no questions asked, that amount with a twenty-five percent finder's fee added. Would you be interested in finding it for us?"

As Larry asked his question he slid a printout of a photo of a lavish diamond necklace with a matching pendant featuring a very large solitaire. A side bar description noted; Archival photograph of Tiffany & Co.'s most important jewel at the 1889 Paris Exposition, the Hazelnut necklace, priced at $150,000.

# Chapter 13

The good evenings were taken care of with Walt and Suz indicating they would consider the offer to go treasure hunting for Walt's previous employer. He started up the Wrangler and they headed down the faint track that defined the road back to what had moments ago thought to be home for them both for the next few years. Twilight was giving way to nightfall and as they approached the difficult section of the road Walt had turned on the head-lights. Neither had spoken since leaving the cabin, both lost in their own thoughts as to how this new opportunity would affect their relationship. It was now so important to each of them that any threat of risking what had just come their way was unthinkable.

As they entered the downhill pitch with the steep cliff, now off the driver's side of the jeep, Suz uttered the single word question, "Well?" Walt waited until he had successfully managed the difficult section, took a quick look at Suz and answered, "When I am laying in bed with you tonight, with you in my arms, I will give you my thoughts."

Several minutes went by and only the rumble of the jeep tires on the dirt and rocky road bed broke the si-lence. Walt started another conversation. "I am sure you like Larry. He is a little young for this position with what I will call the Company, but make no mistake about this, he was instructed to make contact with us and try to enlist us in a recovery type program. Whether that was the real reason we will find out soon enough. I couldn't be sure of what the contact would be but I was sure it would come. That was what having the gun was all about. If he had stepped out of his jeep with a gun in his hand I would know I was to be, as they now call it, disappeared. That is the world I have left and I don't intend to ever go back anywhere near to that part of it again."

Suz sat silent and didn't speak again until they pulled into the campground and parked next to the van. She exited the Wrangler and came around to the driver's side as Walt stepped out. Standing in front of him and looking into his eyes she spoke in a whisper, "I will spend the night here with you. Love you as that is what I want and need right now, but you will have to convince me nothing like what you are suggesting will ever happen. I must have your promise. It must never happen!"

Suz was true to her word and after Walt had gone through his nightly routine of searching his email for things that might be important and browsing those that piqued his interest he closed up his iPad. As he entered the bedroom section of the van he saw Suz siting on the bed cross legged, dressed only in a T-shirt and panties. Her hair was slightly mused and the light was just right to make her tanned skin glow. Her head was down as she was reading something on her iPad. She looked like a painting by an artist who was in love with her. A beautiful sight that took his breath away leaving him frozen in place and staring at her as she looked his way and smiled.

Words were not needed. They both knew at that moment that nothing could come between them and they would be together from that moment on, no matter what might face them in the future.

Walt then spoke of his thoughts about the intertwining of Mary White and Mabel Normand, and that the young Prince's gift of the necklace to her had to be related. It was bringing them closer together and into a group that would be important to them in the future. That tomorrow they could look forward to the next steps in what now seemed to be underway.

Promptly at 10:00 the next morning the knock came on the van's door and Jack was looking up at Walt who was dressed in shorts, sans shirt, and barefoot. Without any embarrassment he posed that Mary White was hoping they could join her at 11:30 for an early lunch. She had some things she wanted them to look at and several to give to them. The invitation was accepted by Walt, knowing Suz would definitely want to have some more time with her newly adopted grandmother.

Mary's greeting was again special as she was now sure she had some new, young friends that would see her through her last years. She also knew things they needed to know, even though they didn't realize what they were, as they did their initial research into the life of Mabel Normand. It was Suz that would think she knew her secret, and suspected Walt probably might be thinking it as well.

They had lunch which was prepared and served by her young caregiver, Alice Bryant. She was also becoming part of Mary's family as Jack had been for years and who was now being brought back more closely into her sphere. Things were falling into place with reliving this most exciting time of her life. Even Ollie was back and just the day before had asked her to marry him again for the thousandth time.

Mary White realized she was happy. Happy again after she had thought only a week ago she was just waiting around to die.

After lunch the chairs were drawn around Mary's big recliner and she placed a fairly large, flat box on her lap. She lifted the top off and it was filled with old black and white photos and a number of newspaper clippings. The photo on top was of her parents with a five year old Mary standing between them. It took only one glance by Suz to see the  resemblance of Mary White as a child to a young Mabel Normand. The shinning dark eyes alone were enough to make the conclusion that she  could  have been Mabel's daughter.

Mary made no comment about the photo but looking at Suz said, "You were thinking this yesterday when you looked at the photos on my wall, weren't you?" nodding her head in the direction of the collection behind her. "I could see it in your eyes and the smile you gave me when you left."

Walt had been thinking the same thing but said nothing. Ollie had known what had happened for years but had kept Mary's secret. Mary decided now was the time it needed to be shared with her new family.

# Chapter 14

Mary asked Alice to take a break as she needed to speak of things privately about her past that she wanted to be shared with only this small group. Ollie had been told long ago and she was sure that Jack had probably had figured it out. It was to her new acquaintances, Suz and Walt, she wanted to confide in as it was something she was sure, for some reason, that they needed to know about.

Alice seemed to take no offense at being asked to leave and asked Mary how long she had before returning. Mary smiled and told two hours would be long enough. To just be back in time to help her prepare for her afternoon nap.

"Suz, you and Walt think you know what I am about to tell you but you don't." Mary said this as she sifted through the box and lifted out a small, letter sized folder. Opening it exposed a number of newspaper clippings, most headed with the Los Angeles Times motif, which were yellow with age and worn by being read many times by her over the years. The one on top read, September 18, 1926 with the heading capitalized: WEDDING STIRS FILMLAND and the first line italicized: *Elopement of Mabel Normand and Lew Cody on spur of Moment Surprises Thrilling Film Drama.* The column continued on making for a lengthy article.

In one of Mabel's comments was, "I love Lew -

that's all. We have been wonderful friends for years. And last night he proposed and I accepted him." Cody, the next morning as toastmaster at the Breakfast Club is reported saying, "Fellows, I went to a party last night. -- It was my wedding party. I married Mabel Normand."

Mary had handed the page to Suz and she read on through the article reading aloud when something struck her as special. The rest sat mesmerized and watched the emotions show on her face as the story was told.

Mary then passed the second article to her. Again it was headed by the Los Angeles Times motif dated February 16, 1927. In bold print it's headline was: Doctors Hurry Mabel Normand Into Hospital.  It was followed by two short paragraphs including the hospital, Santa Monica, and the attending physicians Dr. H. C. Loos, her family physician, and Dr. George Dazey of  Santa Monica. The illness was cited as a bronchial affliction that threatened to develop into pneumonia.

Suz read the two, short paragraph descriptions and looked up towards Mary. She smiled looking at Suz, then at Walt and Jack. She nodded her head toward Ollie and said in a whisper, "My birthday is recorded as February 17, 1927 and that afternoon it was reported that Mabel Normand was feeling better. It would be March 28, however, before she was able to leave the hospital. She had actually been very ill. Mabel fought off this illness for three more years and then died in February, 1930 from tuberculosis. Lew passed away in 1934 from a stroke. She, and they, could have been good parents for me if they and fate had chosen that path. They, and it, didn't however. They were good people."

Mary suddenly looked tired and none present were

sure what, at that moment, should be done for her. She then straightened up her posture and with a renewed sense of purpose stated, "I will now tell you what actually happened on my birth day."

It was a nice story of good people doing good things. By 1926 Mary's mother and father had been with Mabel Normand for over fifteen years, always in the background but important to her in many different ways. Her father fixed things. Physical things that were needed to keep the cameras rolling and downtime at a minimum. Her mother was a friend, probably as close to Mabel as any in a personnel way. Never in the spotlight but always present when she needed help or hope.

As the years went by the Mabel Normand brand had become famous and the requirement of more and better began to take it's toll. The feisty, petite five foot one star was meeting with early aging and health issues and the need for stand-ins became more important. Her favorite was a tall girl, almost seven inches taller than her, but who was a remarkable look a like for many shoots and special athletic stunts. Margret Turner was probably not her real name and she seemed not to have any family or close friends other than Mabel.

At the time of Mabel and Lew Cody's marriage she found herself pregnant and was determined to have and keep her child even if out of wedlock. Mabel was her support but the events in February, 1927 threw all their plans into chaos. Mabel's deteriorating health had her ask, and then plan, for Mary's mother to be the child's God mother and she would provide all the financial needs for this special friend of hers. Mary's birth on February 17 appeared normal until the very last stage of delivery when Margret began to hemorrhage. Later it would be determined it was pre-eclampsia of which she had had some minor symptoms but were not recognized by the doctors. She died within a few hours of giving birth. A rushed adoption, desired by the childless Smiths, was initiated by Mabel's legal team and quickly accomplished.

It was a Charles Russell painting that Mabel had purchased, just a year before Russell's death, that she had given Mary's father that had him dreaming of living in Wyoming or Montana. And that was where Mary, some ninety years later, was now sitting in her big chair surrounded by her new family.

Alice knocked on the door and entered the small room asking if it was time for her to be there. Mary said yes and put the clippings folder back in the box and placed it's top back on. She handed it to Suz, told her to take it home and go through what had been saved and see if she could find what it was she and Walt were looking for.

A luncheon would be planned for the small group as guests of Ollie's at his  home as soon as Mary felt ready for more remembrances of the past. He asked her to marry him one more time. At least once more was left as a promise and she gave him another of her best smiles as she said her good afternoons to Ollie and the rest.

# Chapter 15

Lunch at Ollie's was planned for two days later and all were excited about the events that seemed to be forming around this small group of new friends. That afternoon Walt and Suz went through Mary's box of memories. Walt took the photographs and Suz the printed documents. Both ordered their items chronologically as best they could starting with the dated material. It became apparent that after March of 1927 little was left to sort through except a letter sized box which had letters from Mabel to Mary's mother on a once a month spacing until mid-1929. Interestingly, almost all the letters were written in a combination of English and French.

They sat on the bed and as it became covered they talked about minor discoveries and fun tidbits. Suz finally said the obvious, "I wanted Mabel to be Mary's mother. It would have made such a nice story to think that she had had a child. Someone to leave her genes and history with. To die leaving no one behind is so sad."

Walt could see the tears forming and reached over to touch her arm. "We should have known it was the case as Mabel was five foot one and Lew Cody was only five ten. Mary was five eight, probably even a bit taller, when a young woman. She looks much smaller now but still is not little. What we had in the way of information on Mabel's last years made it a possibility but the physical sizes should have indicated it was not probable. Lew apparently loved her and he did what he could to be with her until the end. Tuberculous was not a disease one could ignore back then and he also had illnesses that were serious enough to be careful with. The idea they never consummated their marriage, as reported by some biographers, seems some what doubtful to me as I suspect they must have had at least some intimate moments together."

It was time for dinner and they decided to walk to the Village Cafe for a hamburger, fries and a beer. Jack was there with two men in rough clothing and freshly sun burnt skin. An early morning deer hunt had not been successful but they had spotted the trophy they would try for the next morning. They were just finishing their dinner and excused themselves from Jack who came over to Suz and Walt's table and took the invite to take a seat.

"Those two have hunted together every season for years and this, they say, will be their last hunt. They no longer need a kill for meat and even the idea for a trophy has lost most of it's appeal. It happened to me ten years ago, for Ollie some twenty odd years ago, especially after Mary's husband passed away. They were best friends. Do either of you hunt?" was a question he let hang over the conversation.

It was Suz that answered first. "I went on one hunt with my husband. It was for antelope, maybe a hundred miles to the east of here on the Colorado, Wyoming border. We had a buck/doe license for husband and wife. He shot his buck, field dressed it and was dragging it back to our jeep when a doe walked up in front of me, about thirty yards away, stopped and stood there looking at me. I shot it and I still can't forget that look. I never went hunting again and he gave it up after one more deer hunt the following season."

Walt could sense Suz and Jack were waiting for his answer and he didn't want to tell them what he was thinking at the moment. It suddenly occurred to Suz that she knew why he hesitated and she reached for his hand as she remembered the body cam images of the three men, on a boat in a gray sea, toppling overboard as the gunfire rang in her ears. He said simply that he had never hunted any game animals and didn't think he would start now at this time in his life.

Jack sensed the awkwardness at the table and changed the subject a bit to the times he and Ollie had scouted for big horn sheep. He started with the Mutt and Jeff image of his six foot two and the five foot seven Ollie. They would make long scouting hikes up into the higher peaks to give them vast areas to glass. They would carry day packs, each with water, food, binoculars, a spotting scope, rain jackets, flashlights, and down vests. Jack's stride was long at a slow cadence and frequent rest stops. Ollie's was short with a faster cadence and he took no breaks. Every five hundred yards, or so, he would be  fifty yards ahead of Ollie, would stop to take a breather and would hear Ollie approaching from below. Soon he would be next to him and with quick glance his way would continue on up the slope. Jack would then catch up and pass Ollie until another fifty yards of separation was  made and while he rested Ollie would continue on by and never stop this routine until they had reached the spot they wanted to glass from. "Ollie could out hike any man living, always knew exactly where he was and never get lost. Even in a dense forest and after dark, he could find his way back to the camp or the car."

The affection that Jack had for Ollie could not be missed. It was not a son to father but a friendship of equals even with more than two generations in years of separation.

Once back in the van Walt and Suz started to place the files and photographs back in the box. Suz showed a newspaper page to Walt and said, "Take a close look at the dark eyed girl next to the Prince."

"There's our necklace. A nightclub scene in Paris, France, September 4, 1922. How convenient," said Walt as he placed the photos in the box and then added Suz's pile leaving the newspaper with the diamond necklace around Mabel Normand's pretty neck on the top of the pile. There was no pendant with a very large solitaire mounted in a cluster design of small diamonds, but the thirteen solitaires joined by distinctive and identical designed clusters made the identification easy.

After they had readied for bed and snuggled up close Suz whispered in Walt's ear, "I wonder where the pendant is now. At the bottom of the side bar on the photograph Larry showed us it says that the necklace had disappeared and probably its diamonds were reset in other jewels. Do you think there is more than just finding that necklace that is being asked of you?"

"I am not sure but we won't go very far with this until I find out what it is they are really after. I can't think that it is just the monetary value. There must be more to it than that," was Walt's unsatisfactory answer.

# Chapter 16

The next day was spent with a pleasant start waking up slowly together in bed. Breakfast in the van of dry cereal and fruit was finished off with hot coffees taken out to the bench overlooking the river. They sat close to each other, the touching sending the unspoken signals of lovers to each other. The early Fall morning was perfect in temperature, with clear skies and the flowing of water below them adding to the magic.

Walt finally stood and pulled Suz up into his arms for a long embrace. He then suggested it would be a nice time to wander about the town and see if there were things they should investigate right here in their new world. Maybe leave that other world for later in the day, or just forget about it until tomorrow.

They ended up at the golf course shortly after noon and had hot dogs, potato chips and a Pepsi for lunch. They tasted as good as any they had had at other courses and shared a candy bar for dessert. A game was set for next week as Walt thought his wound would be healed by then and they both wanted to play.

The afternoon was spent in the van, on-line researching for some connection between Prince Ibrahim, Mabel Normand, the necklace and today. Current news from Egypt and Sudan didn't find any prospects. In the Sudan there was nothing but war and hardship. There seemed to be nothing good in North Africa, or for that matter anywhere else. Dubois, Wyoming was looking better and better. Just as Suz was closing down her iPad a link showed up on the screen that showed a very interesting necklace that looked vaguely familiar. It was there, blinked and then disappeared. She touched the back arrow but the previous page was the one she had just closed when the image had appeared. Closing the page a second time was normal and she closed down the device deciding to not mention this brief image to Walt as she was not sure she had actually seen it.

Later in the evening they took their coffees to their now favorite bench to watch the river go by and the sun set behind the towering peaks to the west. Once back in the van, preparing for sleep laying close together, Walt asked in a whisper, "You saw it too, didn't you?"

Suz moved even closer to Walt and he could feel her begin to shake. "What is going on? How can they, whoever they are, access us so easily? What do they really want?" she asked with a tremor in her voice.

Walt was quiet and Suz waited as she let his hand massage her shoulder in a comforting manner, but not asking for anything more.

"I have no idea but I don't think it is just the necklace but something that it is connected with it that they don't want known. Or at least not known of to the public. We won't find out what that is until we have the necklace in hand," Walt answered and Suz could detect the uncertainty in his voice that made her even more uneasy.

"Maybe we shouldn't go there at all. Not make anymore searches and leave that piece of jewelry where ever it is. I think we should look for something different for us to do," Suz saying this as she tried to get even closer to Walt and waited for him to give her the comforting hug she was needing.

The next morning dawned the same as the day before and by eleven o'clock they were walking, with Jack, on the path along the river towards Ollie's house for lunch and their first look at the private domain of their new friend.

From the outside Ollie's house looked like many others along the river bank. Aged board and bat construction, a more modern steel roof and an expansive veranda porch. On the porch were Ollie, Mary with her walker and Alice. All smiling and waving a come up and join us welcoming.

They were invited inside before Walt and Suz could adequately admire the wonderful view of the Wind River stretching in both directions before them but what was inside made up for the hurried entrance. The large main room was like a high end art gallery. Numerous paintings and sculptures in the best of western traditional art and both of the new guests recognized the fine collection of Russell and Remington works. There were five Russell paintings, two of his sculptures, with the several Remington's placed about in a fine display of some of their best works.

"Charlie Russell was a good friend of my father's and would always stop for a visit whenever he was going through town. He died, at sixty-two, just about the time I was born so I never got to meet him. I wish he had stayed around a little longer but I do have the nice collection of his work thanks to my father. Look over there on the post." Ollie proudly saying this as he pointed to it.

By this time all had glasses of wine in hand,  again poured from an unlabeled bottle, and had formed a half circle around the post. There hung a nicely framed letter with three miniature paintings by Russell and thanking Ollie's father for the nice stay and the good conversation. Even the included envelope had a tiny cowboy painted in one corner having a broad smile on his face.

Suz was taken by what this indicated about what Ollie's parents must have been like and that reflected on Mary's as they had all been close friends. In this small town on the bend of a river she had much more to learn about and she was thinking that maybe this was where she should be. Belonging somewhere was a new sensibility for her and she was beginning to understand its value.

Lunch was braised venison fillets served with wild rice and diagonally sliced carrots. A delicious one plate meal was set at Ollie's big table. It was a good group as was the conversation. Dessert was Dove ice cream bars served on a silver platter by the smiling host.

After lunch Mary asked Alice to play a few pieces on Ollie's parlor grand piano for them to enjoy as they wandered about his gallery like living room. The spell was broken by Suz's audible gasp and her calling for Walt to come over to see what she had just found.

In an old and worn looking shadow box frame, under a smokey glass cover, was a rather large and unusual necklace. Mary, using her walker, rattled her way over as fast as she could. "You know that necklace. I was sure you would!" was excitedly addressed to Suz. "Paris in 1922 with Prince Ibrahim. You know of this story but not why it was so important for me and my mother and father."

# Chapter 17

Mary organized the group quickly with Alice clearing the table, Ollie covering it with a small blanket and having Suz place the shadow box on the blanket. She had Suz sit to her right and as Alice backed away, invited her to join the group on her left. The boys were directed to sit opposite the girls.

It was organized quickly and none had any chance to do anything other than do what had been asked. Mary placed her hand on the box and said nothing for almost a minute. Then in a voice trembling with emotion she said, "This is the reason we are sitting here together. This necklace, what is left of it, is what made my life what it has been. Without it my life would have been lived but would have turned out much different. It is what it has been and I have no regrets. It is why we are here together. The why is another story, one I don't know yet but it has to do with why Suz and Walt have joined us. That we can find out about later."

Another long pause, then Mary said, 'Let me tell you a story."

It started with her father finding employment in the silent film industry, and later her mother joining the same studio, in Southern California. It was Mabel Normand that had brought them together and it was she that had her being adopted by her parents as a new born orphan. It was the relationship of Mabel with her mother that brought them together this afternoon.

"My mother loved Mabel as a kindred soul. She told me many times that she was the smartest and most intelligent person she had ever known. Short, at just over five foot, but the tallest of any in any place or situation. Kindly and generous to a fault. She did drink and could out swear most but would agonize about any slight or hurt she might cause to anyone. She was a Catholic. A good one about most things but lived a life that was full beyond the teachings of the church. She had had little formal education but was an avid reader of books. Serious books carefully selected, read and understood. She could speak and write in both English and French and during their friendship my mother also became fluent in French."

Mary had to take a break as this relationship with Mabel was closer than her mother had had with any other in her life. Mabel's early death had haunted her the rest of her life but it had, however, secured her family's life here in Wyoming. It was because of this unusual necklace that now sat on the table in the strange shadow box beneath the smoky glass that hid it's beauty and mystery.

Mary reached forward and pulled the box closer to her, releasing the four small hook type clasps on each end of the long sides of the box. She then slowly lifted the box off the base that held the necklace on a dark blue velvet form. A gasp came from each in the room, except for Mary and Ollie as they knew what was hidden under the smoky glass cover. The overhead light hit the jewelry and the sparkling tiny diamonds, diamond chips and platinum filigree of the four leaf clusters seemed to fill the room with a luminous glow. They were linked together, almost invisibly, with thirteen empty diamond settings making up the necklace. The settings for the missing diamonds, the largest at the bottom, rose in six reduced sizes on each side up to the top most four leaf cluster that hid the clasp. The clusters were also proportioned in reduced sizes matching those of the diamond settings.

For a moment all sat quietly, mesmerized by what lay before them. Ollie then stood and told them to not move because he had one thing to add before the spell should be broken. He left the room and was soon back wearing thin, white cotton gloves holding a small, very old paper envelope and emptied it's content into his free hand. He quickly position and set the 5 carat diamond in the bottom setting and snapped it into place.

"My God, look at that! Unbelievable! Just unbelievable," was Suz's whispered exclamation. She had taken from her pocket a folded letter sized paper, unfolding it and placing it next to the necklace. It was a copy of page 69 in Tiffany Diamonds, by John Loring. A photograph of the necklace they had before them and in addition showed a large, matching pendant hanging below it sporting a much bigger diamond than those of the necklace.

Now all at the table gasped at what had been presented. Even Mary and Ollie as they had never known the pendant had even existed. On the side of the page was a typed description. Suz read it aloud as Walt watched her, marveling at how effortlessly she could present such value to what had just been revealed.

"Archival photograph of Tiffany and Company's most important jewel at the 1889 Paris Exposition, the Hazelnut necklace, priced at $150,000. The pendant's 25.09 carat central diamond had a troubled history. Paris's leading gem dealer, Joseph Halpern, sold it to Turkish sultan Abdul Aziz, who gave it as a wedding present to a member of Egypt's viceregal family. Upon Egypt's bankruptcy in 1875-76, the ousted Ismail Pasha sold it back to Halpern, who ran into financial difficulties of his own and resold it to Tiffany's. This necklace has disappeared: presumably its diamonds were reset in other jewels."

Ollie smiled at this as he, and Mary, knew what had happened to the thirteen main stones on Mary's necklace. Also, one of those was sparkling in front of them. It was Mary's story, so Ollie waited.

"You all know the story of my adoption and within a year Mabel's health had started to decline in earnest. By March, 1929 she was placed in a sanitarium and died less than a year later on February 23, 1930.

"She had promised she would help my mother and father with the expenses in raising me and it was during this time, knowing she was dying, that she gave my mother the necklace and told her to use the diamonds to cover any costs they couldn't afford."

Mary had to stop as the tears had come and her sadness couldn't be hidden. Ollie offered to take her home if she was tired and needing rest. She smiled back with a look that couldn't be mistaken for anything but love.

"No! I have one more story you must hear before this day is over. That is how Mabel had this necklace in her collection. How it got there," Mary said this quickly with a new burst of energy. "Mabel was in Paris in June until early September, 1922. She was being romanced by Prince Ibrahim and they were doing all the sights and parties available to the rich and famous. Parties, road trips, night clubs and outings all being covered by the ever present press. When he came to pick her up at her hotel, for what was to be this last time in Paris, he presented the necklace for her to wear that evening."

Mary stopped and was obviously thinking of something about what she was about to tell them. "Now I understand something I had forgotten. Mabel had told my mother this story many times and she had retold it to me several times as I grew older. The prince placed it around Mabel's neck and fixed the clasp. The pendant hung too low on Mabel's chest, she giggled and told him it was scratching her between her breasts. He took it off, removed the pendant stuffing it in his pocket, and replaced the necklace as before. Mabel said she kept the necklace but never saw the pendant again!"

Walt calmly said, "A twenty-five carat Tiffany diamond stuffed in his pocket and they were off to do the Paris party scene. Maybe it is lost forever."

# Chapter 18

It had been an exciting afternoon of revelations and emotional remembrances. The new family bonds were growing stronger between them and the ancestral history was enjoyable to both talk of and learn. Mary said it was time for her to rest a bit at home and the formalities were taken for goodbyes but Ollie had asked Walt and Suz to remain a while longer.

He popped out the diamond, replaced it in the small packet and, with the necklace in hand, motioned Walt and Suz to follow him into the room that was his office. Like the main room, there was no doubt about being what he called it, an office. In the back corner was a big, built in safe. The safe door was open and he placed the small packet in a narrow box that had a number of like packets standing in a row. Thirteen, to be exact, but not that could be counted from a distance.

Another box was taken out with the beautiful Tiffany name in a large scroll on the top. It was old but still could be thought of as in good condition. He lifted the lid and removed what was obviously an inexpensive copy of the necklace he held in his other hand. Having removed the copy he replaced it with the genuine one, made a few minor adjustments and replaced the top. He put the box back on the shelf in the safe where it had been, closed the safe's door and spun the dial. Walt could see from where he was standing that there was a place for the missing pedant on the dark blue velvet form which was now back in the safe.

He guided his guests back into the living room, placed the copy in the shadowbox, positioned the top and secured the four clasps. He then hung the box in it's place on the post. Turning he looked at his startled guests and asked if they had left their cell phones in the van or if they had them with them.

Walt looked at Ollie, then Suz as he took his cell phone and placed it on the table. She knew that Walt was obeying a request, not just answering a question, and did the same.

"Let's take a walk down to the river's edge. It is a nice place to talk about the many things that seem to be bringing us together," was said in a voice that Walt had not heard from Ollie until that moment but had heard many times before from others. A look into Ollie's eyes told him this wasn't just a small old man nearing the end of his life. Old he may be but his mind was still sharp and he would be telling them what they should know if they were thinking of looking for the pendant and what it might mean if they found it. Suz had taken Walt's hand and was squeezing it so tight that he was sure she knew what was happening and was ready, even if not wanting,  to find out what it was.

They sat at a picnic table near the river, with Ollie's back to it and Walt and Suz facing him. He smiled and his eyes sparkled. "You have heard, at least, the best part of the story. Mary's mother's time with Mabel Normand, her birth, the circumstance of her adoption and the gift of the necklace to help support the family. How I got here, sitting here talking to you, is not that important but I need to give you at least an idea."

Ollie smiled with an almost impish grin and continued, "As a kid I never knew exactly what Mary's parents did to make a living but her mother taught at the one room school house."

Again Ollie paused as he was trying to set the up the close relationship of the two families over the years until the obvious end that was coming for the only children of the two couples that had formed it.

"It was as the depression deepened that Mary's parents moved up here from Los Angeles and mine had arrived earlier. You should understand what a small town Dubois was back then. In 1910 F. A. Welty's was the first real general store here and any supplies, other than basic food stuff, came from Omaha, first by train and then the last hundred miles by horse drawn wagons. It took two weeks. Ten years later the first cars began showing up and by the time I was born Welty's had expanded and even had a gas pump. The town literally grew up around the general store. Sometime later the highway was paved and Jackson Hole became a destination to reach the southern entrance of Yellowstone National Park. The depression and World War II, of course, slowed everything down."

Ollie then settled into telling an another bit of Dubois history. "Two men, George Cassidy and Al Hainer, came here in 1889, buying a horse ranch that then seemed to be selling more horses than could be raised. They only lasted as horse breeders a year. One of the local bankers noted that George once made a deposit of $17,500, which was a very large sum for that time. George Cassidy later became known by the a nickname, 'Butch.'"

Suz joined Walt in enjoying the story as they could understand why Ollie had told it. Suz commented with laughter in her voice, "1889, now let me guess, that was the year our necklace was first displayed at the Paris Exposition. Tiffany's most important jewel at the time, priced at $150,000 was the top draw. I bet your short term residents would liked to have been in Paris then."

"Other than Mary and Jack, I have no one left to tell my stories to." Ollie then continued,"I always hope they have more to them than just the story. You both seem to see it immediately this time and that makes you victims for more. Don't let me become a boring old man. Although the old part I can't help."

"Mary, about three years old, and her parents arrived in their 1927 Chevrolet four door in 1930. Why they stopped in Dubois I never understood but it may have been just fatigue from driving. They took a room at the Ramshorn Hotel and the next day looked for a house to rent. The Welty's owned a small house that was vacant and a discussion as to rent versus owning ended up them buying it. That is the house where Mary is now residing."

"My parents came west from Chicago in 1920, started a bakery in Lander, then later moved here and started a second one. I showed up in 1930 to complicate their life but things worked out good for our family. I was born two months early, was little and stayed that way never making it to five foot eight. But I was a tough little squirt and took no insults without a fight. I usually lost but soon no one bothered me." Ollie stopped with this as Walt and Suz could see him remembering some of the things in his youth he could not forget.

"I went to Dartmouth College, graduated in four

years with honors as a business major and came home. My years in the service were limited as they didn't need me, being a bit short and having a heart tick had me discharged early. A top downhill ski racer for four years at Dartmouth didn't count."

Ollie put his hands out on the table, straightened up and got to the point of having them come out of the house and talk.

"My mother also helped run the one room school and both Mary and I graduated the same year. I skipped two years. I was pretty smart and loved school. Every year or two Mary's father would travel, by himself for a week or two, then return never telling anyone where he had gone or what he was doing. He was a fix it man and could fix or repair anything that wasn't alive. Incredibly smart. I actually think he was a genius."

Again Ollie fell silent and Walt and Suz could see something was causing him trouble to speak about was coming. "My father was a jack of all trades and made his living practicing that. He was also a hunter and guide with a reputation as a top bighorn sheep guide which had him making top dollars guiding the rich and famous on hunts. He bought his first airplane in 1935 and taught himself to fly. He talked a friend who had some flat land into letting him build an airstrip and a crude hangar on it. It was while I was in college that he was scouting for some out of the way bighorn herds that he made the mistake of flying too low into a box canyon and couldn't fly his way up and out of it. It took two weeks to find the crash site and it was decided to bury him there, up in the mountains he loved."

Again Ollie fell quiet and brushed the tears from his face. "My mother, two years later, sold the bakeries and moved to live with her sister in Chicago. I saw her very little after that. Here I now sit, nearing the end, a hundred yards from where I was born."

He then hit the table hard enough to rattle one of the loose boards and brought back Walt and Suz from thinking about all that he had just told them.

"The necklace and it's lost pendant! Isn't it amazing that a lost 1889 Tiffany diamond necklace has us sitting here with me telling you, almost strangers, my and Mary's life stories. You know the start of this and I will fill you in on what I know about the necklace up to this point. Then it is in your court and I am finished with it!"

# Chapter 19

It was a pretty place near the river, the trees beginning to show the first signs of Fall and the sounds muted by the geography of the place. Ollie had gone silent and Walt and Suz were respecting his silence. He was looking around the surroundings that had been his home for most of his life. His eyes betrayed a sadness of knowing his time was now limited, thinking he hadn't done all things he had wanted to do and that he had at least one more needing his attention.

"Now!" he stated sharply to break the spell, "What it is I want you two to do for me. For us, maybe all of us. It was about sixty years ago that Mary's father approached me one day and suggested we come down to this table and talk for a bit. He had a sad look on his face and merely said he had been working on a project that he was no longer able to continue, or finish. A simple project to find the pendant that Prince Ibrahim had stuffed into his pocket when the necklace he placed around Mabel Normand's neck, with it attached, was uncomfortable for her."

He explained that Mabel, as her health was deteriorating, had given the necklace to them to help support themselves while raising their newly adopted daughter. To sell the solitaire diamonds one at a time as needed. There were no strings attached, the monitory value was of no importance to her and no reporting necessary to her of the results. It was pure generosity, so uncommon in this world, was how Mary's father had described this life changing gift to Ollie.

"I followed up with selling diamonds eleven and twelve for them but went no farther. A simple trip to Chicago first and a second one to New York. It was after my trip to New York, that was in the 1960s, I think, after Mary had graduated from the University of Colorado and had married. It was to help them start their new life together with no debts and a nest egg for their future. The Eisenhower recession of 1958 was underway and her mother and father were having some financial problems of their own. The proceeds from number twelve helped carry them all through to it's end. It was the day after Mary's father's funeral that I received a call from a person I have only heard from that one time. He only said not to pursue anything I might find in Mary's inheritance that had to do with a Tiffany necklace. Don't sell the last diamond and do not to pursue searching for the pendant. He finished with telling me my life would be much better, and last much longer, if I heeded his advice. He then hung up."

Ollie's face took on a blank expression and seemed to turn gray in the late afternoon light. Walt spoke in an almost whisper, "You were right not to do anything more on this. I have been approached by a party that wants to start this search again and the situation appears equally ominous. It is through an organization I worked for the last ten years and it is the locating of the necklace that is why we are here at this moment. It has something to do with the pendant, however, not the necklace in your safe."

Again it appeared there was nothing to be said at the moment but then Ollie, in a quiet tone offered, "I think you both see what is happening in our country, and world-wide, right now. It is not good and bodes very poorly for the future. The year I was born the population of Dubois was one hundred seventy-seven according to the census that year. Ten years later four hundred twelve and in 1950 it was back down to two hundred seventy nine. The 2000 census counts only nine hundred sixty-two. A small town in a big county in a big state. Fremont County is the same size New Hampshire in size and had only thirty-five thousand in population in 2000."

They sat in silence and let the beauty of the place quell their thoughts of what had just been said. Ollie looked at Suz, then toward Walter and continued, "I was a little guy in a world of big ones. At first picked on but those who teased me soon found out it was not a wise thing to do. I may have got beaten up but they felt the pain that small, hard fists could deliver. It was not long that I was accepted as an equal and had no more problems unless someone had forgotten what a mean little boy I could be. Only my mother ever saw me cry and she always did her best to comfort me. I think I have had an extraordinarily good life and it has been a good time to be alive. I have no way to fight against what I see coming and it will be your generation that will have to take care of it for mine." Ollie stood giving a nod to Walt and Suz, told them he had a gift for them up at the house and not to forget their phones left on the table. When they were inside he went to his bookcase and retrieved one of the two The Classic Guide To Fly-Fishing For Trout, written by Charles Jardine.

As he handed it to Suz he said he thought they both would enjoy reading through it, the author stopped for a visit anytime he was in the area and they often spent a few hours on the river. He was a master at fly-fishing and he hoped he would make at least one more visit. "If he does the four of us will wet a line together as he would want to meet the best fly-fisherman in Wyoming."

Ollie found a cloth grocery bag in the kitchen, put an unlabeled bottle of wine, a letter size folder in it and then had Suz add the large book. He handed the bag to Walt, and Walt and Suz said their thank yous, good afternoons and took their leave.

Walt and Suz walked along their favorite route along the river, holding hands but not talking. It had been an exciting afternoon as much had been spoken of and even more had been left unsaid.

Suz suddenly stopped and turned to face Walt, quickly saying, "It is happening, isn't it! We are being drawn into something that is much bigger than can be imagined. Here in this tiny place, we by chance, are now involved in something no one knows what but which must be done. Should we do this?"

Walt looked directly into her eyes and with no hesitation answered, "Yes!"

# Chapter 20

Once they were back in the van the decision was made to sort out what Ollie had given them. Walt told Suz exactly what she was also thinking. That he had put in the bag what they would need to start their journey of discovery. The beautiful book on fly-fishing and the bottle of wine were a cover if anyone other than the three of them was observing this contact. Even if it had been decades since he was involved with the necklace, and the pendant, Ollie had been warned in a way that had him back away from any more involvement.

"What was going on back then that would involve a missing diamond pendant and then be of importance again now?" Walt asked expecting no answer.

"I am going to go fishing first and you can have the folder that probably has the important papers," was Suz's response to Walt and she pulled the big book out of the bag. The book jacket was like new and on the first page was a note to Ollie expressing a thank you from the author and also the acknowledgment that he was being given two books, this one to be given to a friend when the time was right. The signature of Charles Jardine was bold and had a nice flourish.

Walt took out the bottle of wine and offered it to Suz. She took a quick glance and indicated the refrigerator would be a good place to put it for now and started leafing through the beautiful pages in the book on her lap. Walt put the wine away, took his seat in the second captain's chair and withdrew the slender folder letting the empty bag fall to the floor between the chairs.

The first page was a list of thirteen diamonds numbered one through thirteen. All but the last, thirteen, had notes listing carat, paid amount, date, buyer, location, address, telephone number, deposit date, account, bank, and amount deposited. One through ten were written in very precise lettering and in ink. Eleven and twelve were in pencil, still nice, but in a different hand and were also easily read. Eleven showed selling in Chicago and twelve showed the buyer at Tiffany, New York City. The dates confirmed the last sale by Mary's father and the last sale by Ollie.

Suz remarked that she had just found the Renegade fly on page 128 and read the description to Walt. "It is in the Classics section and listen to this. 'This fly is unusual in that a hackle is placed at the bend of the hook and conventionally to the fore. Jack Dennis, the famous Wyoming fly-tier, rates it as one of the top rainbow trout flies in the West which is recommendation enough'. Ollie's is weighted and the body just a bit longer, but otherwise looks the same."

She looked toward Walt for a reaction and saw an expression she was beginning to recognize. He had found something on the page he was studying that had taken his interest beyond her presence. She waited and he answered, "The last sale Mary's father made of the individual diamonds and the last sale Ollie made were both with Tiffany in New York City. Ollie told us of the phone call he had received after this sale and Mary's father had asked Ollie to handle the remaining three sales after his last sale in New York with the same buyer. We have a place to start and, by my estimate, a five carat Tiffany diamond to sell in New York City."

Walt could see the look of fear on Suz's face and put the paper he was holding back in the folder and picking up the bag, placed them both in the side pocket of the captain's chair. He reached for the book, marked her place with a slip of paper and laid it on the small table, "Let's take the bottle of wine and two glasses down to our favorite bench, drink the wine and let the Wind River tell us what we should do. Maybe it will also tell us why we should and what will happen if we don't."

Suz got up out of her chair and collected the glasses and the cork screw and Walt retrieved the wine bottle with no label. Five minutes later they took their first sips of this fine wine and watched the water passing along over the river bed below them. The sun was setting behind the big mountains and dusk was casting it's long shadows as a big trout started taking it's evening meal, leaving tell-tale rings in a quiet spot in the big river.

Silence seemed best for the moment but after the first glass was emptied and the second filled Walt had leaned forward and picked up a small stone at his feet showing it to Suz. "A quality 26 carat diamond about this size in today's market would bring about a million dollars. Or maybe even twice, or more, than that," Walt said and then closed his hand over it, placed it in his mouth for a moment and then put it into his pocket.

"Big diamonds have always been a way to make wealth portable. Big sums of wealth easily hidden and transported. In the past those in power who had accumulated vast wealth would always convert much of it into gold and diamonds so when deposed they could escape with them. Their castles, villas and land would be left behind but on their person they could escape with enough wealth to live out their remaining years in comfort."

Suz looked at Walt and he waited as he could see that she understood what he was suggesting. "Our diamond may be one of those. Hidden away to be sold later to afford a continued good life. We need to trace those at the time Mary's father, and then Ollie, were threatened," Suz said this with admiration and enthusiasm toward toward Walt who had brought the excitement of the hunt back into her life.

Walt could see this in her eyes and could admire the beauty it brought to her being. The fear that had shown first had quickly tempered and showed that beauty. He knew care was needed because at the moment he had no idea of what they might be facing.

# Chapter 21

Walt stood, set his glass next to the empty bottle on the bench, took Suz's glass placing it next to his and then pulled her up into a comfortable embrace. He kissed her gently on the lips and suggested they return to the van, have something to eat and then plan out a strategy for how to proceed. Suz choose not to move and held Walt to her. She leaned back to look into his eyes, suggesting that tomorrow would be a better time to do the planning and why not just enjoy each other's company for the rest of the evening.

They decided on a bowl cereal topped with fruit for dinner and finished that with small dishes of ice cream. Suz had decided to use the shower and Walt took a peek at his mailbox and wished he hadn't. A short note from Larry Nichols saying that the Hazelnut necklace looked very nice, even without the pendant. To keep in touch, that he had been assigned back to Washington, D.C. but still would be his contact and to reply to this email address.

Walt was staring at the message from Larry when Suz came back from showering wearing only a T-shirt. She took his iPad from him closing it without looking at what he had been reading and put it aside "Tomorrow is the agreement, mister Wainwright," and Walt decided he should honor it.

As they entered the bedroom Suz slipped off  her

T-shirt and turned to face him. The soft lighting in the room made her skin glow with a golden tone and left him almost helpless in making a move toward her. The small gold coin laying above her breasts caught the light in a way that suddenly had his attention. He stepped over to her, lifting it up in his fingertips and asked, "Will you tell me the story about this special coin? Should I know about it?"

Suz smiled and put her arms around his neck, saying, "Yes, and yes. It is about my father and my mother. You need to know and I need you to know. Now is the right time and this is the right place," she said as she pulled him down on the bed to have him next to her as she started her story.

"I was an only child, a California girl, growing up in Manhattan Beach in a nice home within walking distance of the beach. My parents were both professors at UCLA and had most of the perks that professors have at the big universities. They were both good looking, athletic and gave me good mentoring in all that was available. Education, social activities, golf, skiing, surfing, fishing and travel. Lots of travel, including one year living in England while on their sabbaticals taken there at Oxford. Even piano lessons provided that were only partially successful." Suz stopped at this last and Walt waited for what he was expecting was not going to be said so quickly.

"My mother was raised in a strict Catholic family back east and her choice of my father, who claimed no religious belief, as her husband caused a great strain in the family. I was six years old before I first met any of her side of my family. My father's mother and father were atheists although you would never know my father's views on religion unless he was pressed on the subject. Even then you would come away with no objection to his thinking. He was a third generation Californian.

"My mother and father had always seemed to me to be perfectly matched. Looking back I guess I should have sensed some of the signs of what was coming but I was a happy, self-centered young girl and my life couldn't have been better. It was my mother whose life had apparently not matched up to her expectations. My junior year at UCLA I took an apartment shared with a fellow female junior. My senior year roommate would become my husband two years later and I think we had a good marriage going until the car accident that took his life."

"I am still not sure why my mother decided she needed some time on her own that year and went to Europe. In turn, my father decided he wanted to join two other friends to dive for lost 1715 Spanish treasure off the east coast of Florida. This was living aboard a fifty foot luxury yacht and mostly was a vacation with a new diving adventure. Most of the big treasure finds had been made but there was still enough being found to make it a fun project. They planned on three months. It was my last year in college and both my parents promised to be back for my graduation from UCLA that Spring. Neither made it and I didn't attend the ceremonies receiving my diploma by mail."

Again Suz paused and was holding the small coin between her thumb and forefinger, gently massaging it's surface.  Walt could see her face and could tell she was somewhere else remembering things that had her now close to tears. He pulled the sheet up, covering them both, and  gently held her.

"A letter arrived from my mother the end of March, from Florence, Italy, offering an apology for what she had done, that she had found what she hoped was true happiness, wanted her privacy for the time being and provided no contact information. She wished me well and hoped that someday I would be able to understand why she felt as she had to have some time for herself. I still don't understand what happened between them and what happened just one week later was when I received this little coin."  The tears came then and Walt held her tighter and let her have the time she needed.

"It was to be their last week for diving, and other than a few pieces of pottery and one piece of silver from a picked over and abandoned wreck site, they had little to show for their efforts. On the last dive for the day my father surfaced by the swim step, handed his friend this coin and told him that this one was for me."

"They had been diving in fifty feet of water about halfway between Vero Beach and Sebastian, twenty miles off shore. Climbing back aboard he complained of a severe pain in his head and after getting out of his dive gear laid down on one of the cushions, holding his head with both hands, and passed out. His friends didn't know what they should do and they were two hours out from shore so they called for help over the VHF radio. The Coast Guard gave them instructions to come in through the Sebastian Inlet and go to The Cay Marine docks. An ambulance was waiting and he was pronounced deceased at the Sebastian River Medical Center caused by a massive aneurysm. He was only fifty-two years old."

Walt retrieved her T-shirt, helped her into it and positioned them both in bed in a comfortable position for sleeping. Suz's tears had stopped and she held Walt close, her lips against his cheek and whispered in his ear, "The coin is from the 1715 Spanish fleet. It is a one escudos coin, one that had been moved about over the sand by the Gulf Stream current. Probably buried at times for years then back on the surface for a time. My father's friends took it to Mel Fisher's Museum, in Sebastian, and they made the mounting, provided the chain and then mailed it to me. I put it on that day and the only time it was not around my neck were those few minutes behind the Hitching Rack and until you fixed the chain for me."

Suz kissed Walt gently, moved slightly to the position she needed and let sleep come.

# Chapter 22

The next morning following breakfast, with their coffees in hand, they walked down to their now favorite bench and let the river do it's magic. They sat close together, holding hands when Suz softly said, "That was so good of you last night. I needed to tell you my story and  you listened and comforted me.  You are a truly nice person and I want to be with you from now on. Every minute of every day."

Walt acknowledged this with a smile and a long, gentle kiss. They watched the river for a few minutes and then Walt broke the spell saying he wanted to meet with Ollie again. He wanted to have him elaborate on his thinking about things going so badly here. Before he could tell Suz why, she gave him her opinion, "Ollie is a very smart man. Even in his early nineties he is very aware of everything around him. We would be wise to listen to what he has to say about the present and what he knows about the past. What is it you know already, that you can't wait to tell me?" The look and smile she gave him as she asked this question let him know that she was a very smart and wise woman, and that he should always listen to what she had to say.

"So far we have three definite times to study, 1922, 1952 and the last few years. The easy part of the first period is around and about our friend, Prince Ibrahim. The last known location of the necklace's pendant is in his pocket the night he was photographed with Mabel, just before she returned to America. She kept the necklace and brought it back with her. We know where it is at this moment and how it got there. The pendant has another story to tell us and I can only guess about it's path. I think it would be the 25.09 carat diamond that will lead us there."

Walt then started with the Prince, "His full name was Muhammad Ali Ibrahim. He was the great-great grandson of Muhammad Ali Pasha, the head of the Muhammad Ali dynasty. He would then be the second cousin once removed from King Fuad's son, Farouk. Farouk was from King Fuad's second marriage to Nazli Sabri Pasha, who was just six years older than Prince Ibrahim. She has to be the connection to the Tiffany necklace and pendant. King Fuad's reign lasted until his death in 1936 and then Farouk became the king. He would be King until he lost his position in the coup of 1952. It was bookend revolutions, so to speak. Nazli loved collecting jewelry, as did most of the royal women, and I think it was from that collection the Hazelnut necklace was taken by Prince Ibrahim without him knowing, or caring, about it's value. Just another gift to be given to his latest love."

Suz sat silently listening to Walt propose this first step in the search and enjoyed the verbal picture of the young Prince nonchalantly picking up a piece of jewelry from a full jewelry box of like pieces on the King's young wife's dresser. She was probably used to such thievery as the men in her life all had similar traits, that of taking that which wasn't theirs.

She laughed in a pleasant manor then said to Walt,

"Let me tell you about an interesting something I just found online. It is an article in a publication called CEO Magazine. It is titled Inspiring The Business World, dated 28 September 2018 and sub-titled Incredibly Rare 26 carat Fortuna Diamond Unveiled at an Exclusive Event. In the article it describes how a woman unknowingly wore the exquisite 26 carat diamond ring for over three decades, thinking it just costume jewelry after buying it at a London flea market for £10." Suz said all this as in one sentence and then continued with another quote from the article, "If the gem could talk, it would tell amazing stories." With a smile so big she could hardly continue, she sang, "What are the odds, Walter Wainwright! What are the odds!" in the familiar My Fair Lady melody.

Suz brought up the web page and sitting close together they looked through it twice, The photographs were excellent. The one of the diamond mounted as a ring on a women's ring finger showed the circumference and shape of the diamond clearly. It could be thought to be the diamond in the Hazelnut necklace's pendant built by Tiffany. The photo copied from the Tiffany Diamonds book, unfortunately, didn't show the circumference clearly enough to positively reference it to the image in the article's photograph. About a third of the top edge of the Hazelnut diamond did, however, show a reasonable correlation. Also, the weights were different by almost a carat and the newly discovered diamond had been modified slightly to highlight it's brilliance. Still, it was plausible that it could be the Hazelnut diamond and that it would be worth pursing this as a lead.

"We will have to make a date with Ollie for a few hours to talk about what we have found so far. It is a good start and your finding the CEO Magazine coverage is too good to be true, of course, but what a nice coincidence. The London flea market sale would have to have been some where around 1988 so we only have 66 years to have it lost. I think we can at least play around with that in mind," Walt said this and enjoying the speculation decided he would wait until later to mention the email from Larry Nichols.

# Chapter 23

That afternoon Walt and Suz decided a walk along the river would be nice and they would stop by Ollie's house to see if he was there hoping he would have some time for them to talk things over. As they approached his house they could see him sitting on the picnic table down by the river. As they got closer they could see a half filled wine glass next to him and that his posture was projecting a sad and lonely old man. Suz reached for Walt's hand and gave it a squeeze saying to him, "I think he needs someone right now and we will be that someone." Walt looked at her and could see the tears forming in her eyes and returned her squeeze pulling her a little closer.

The path continued just below Ollie's table and as they approached he hadn't moved or indicated he had heard or sensed them being there. Walt called out a greeting and could see his head slowly turn their way but not tell if there was any recognition in his look. "Suz and I are taking a break from hunting for big diamonds, and their owners, and thought you might help us out. Got some time for a visit?" was asked in a cheerful way and they could see the bright eyed look and smile they were hoping for return.

"Good to see you both. I need some company right now. I was musing over my life and realize I need one more endeavor to endeavor. Do you have one handy?" he asked in a way that both Walt and Suz knew they were welcome and that Ollie had time to spend with them. Before they could get seated Ollie suggested they go up to the porch where there was a bottle of wine that needed finishing in the refrigerator and the two glasses needed to help him finish it.

When they stepped up on the porch Ollie asked Suz if she would go inside and retrieve the bottle and glasses for him. As soon as she went inside Ollie turned to Walt and in a serious tone asked him, "Do you understand what a remarkable young woman you have teamed up with? How lucky you are? As smart and intelligent as any woman I have ever met, and beautiful as well. You know this already so you don't have to answer. I know that you match her, at least as far as intelligence goes, and I want you both to be my friends. Let me be part of the quest you are now on. I very badly need something like this, a challenge to exercise my mind a bit."

Walt started to answer but it was then Suz returned with the wine and glasses. They were filled half way and the seating was arranged in a comfortable semi-circle so each had a view of the river below but could easily face the  other when speaking.

Ollie then spoke first. "I was sitting down there contemplating the future of our world and worrying that it wasn't that good. That I was glad to have been alive when I was and that I have been able to make it into old age still able to walk, see, hear, smell, taste and think to enjoy the time I have left. I am afraid we, my generation, are not leaving what we should have for the following generations. I want to tell you what I think happened. Why it has happened and what has gone wrong. This will require a second bottle of wine and a great deal of patience on your part."

Ollie stopped, took a sip from his glass and smiling asked Walt and Suz if he should continue. They nodded their approval, sat back in the chairs and smiled back at this small, elderly man who's eyes now glistened with excitement.

"I will start around 1963. I was living in the San Francisco Bay area and working for a small company that had some sub-contracts with Lockheed Missiles and Space Division. One of my co-workers gave me his Ayn Rand book, Atlas Shrugged, and said I should read it. That it described our future and that we were working for an industry that was part of the problem. It was known as the Military-Industrial Complex as had been described by President Dwight Eisenhower."

"I struggled as Atlas shrugged, but I eventuality made it though the long book. I read each and every word so it took a long time. About that time our youthful students, aided by a few professors and outsiders, over at the University of California formed and promoted the Free Speech Movement with demonstrations and trash talking. Us squares called it the Filthy Speech Movement and it fell somewhere in between."

"The San Francisco Chronicle's popular social columnist was Herbert Caen. He occasionally expressed some political opinions in his columns as did other writers, both sympathetic and otherwise. The opinions that impressed me the most were often offered by Eric Hoffer, known as the Longshoreman Philosopher. He expressed that those kids, they don't know nothing. I found and enjoyed reading a copy of his 1951 book, The True Believer:

Thoughts on he Nature of Mass Movements. It is in my bookcase, over there," saying this as he nodded towards his living room.

Taking an emptying swig of wine from his glass he held it out and waited as Suz, who was nearest the bottle, filled his glass emptying it. Walt stood and went into the house retrieving another with a corkscrew. Ollie smiled and asked him to do the honors and in turn he filled his and Suz's glasses.

Ollie then continued. "It was this movement that warned me that something was wrong. Why would young students make such a fuss about the University taking the position of limiting the amount of political action allowed on campus. Students were there to learn from some of the best educators in the country and that maybe they should listen rather than spout off on political theories they were just learning about. Especially pushing socialism, and more narrowly communism, about what they seemed to know nothing. The experiments in Russia, and later in China, had cost many millions of lives and socialism's cousin, fascism, had demonstrated it's own violence and human sacrilege. It seemed Ayn Rand's capitalism, justifying it with her philosophy of Objectivism, drove these youngster crazy."

"The True Believer sets forth Hoffer's thinking about the motives of the various types of personalities that give rise to mass movements, their rise and fall, and that whether radical or reactionary, tend to always attract the same sort of people. The BLM riots of today are essentially populated by the same types that rioted at the 1968 Democratic Convention."

Ollie paused here for a long moment, then added

"Anyone can ride on a train, only a wise man knows when to get off." Ollie clarified that it was one of Eric Hoffer's many wonderful quotes and added that Hoffer had a favorite rock in one of the San Francisco city parks where he would sit, bundled up in a pea-coat and smoking a cigar, taking interviews and providing many his one line tidbits of philosophic gems. "Early TV news loved him and so did I."

"Now where the hell is this damn diamond we are looking for?"

# Chapter 24

Walt looked around, first to Suz and then to Ollie, thinking that he was no stranger to the writings of Ayn Rand.  He had read all her books and subscribed to her Objectivist philosophy but at this moment thought it would  be  better to just answer Ollie's last question. So he did.

"The diamond we are looking for is the one mounted in the pendant that was once part of the Tiffany necklace, Hazelnut, of about 1889. We know it was in the possession of Prince Ibrahim when he presented it to Mabel Normand in Paris in early September, 1922. He removed the pendant from the necklace at her request and stuffed it into his pocket. The necklace is now in the house on whose porch I am now sitting. And we know how it got there. The pendant's last known location was in the Prince's coat pocket as he and Mabel left for partying that evening. Mabel was wearing the necklace. All the solitaire diamonds of the necklace are accounted for, twelve sold and the last, the  5 carat round, is next to the necklace at this moment. We, the team here in Dubois, all know this but are the only people that do. The pendant, or at least it's 25.09 carat cushion diamond, must be somewhere as diamonds are forever."

Suz then entered the conversation and told Ollie the story they had found about the Fortuna diamond, close to the same size and purchased at a flea market some 35 years ago in London. The story was it was thought to be costume jewelry and had been purchased for twelve dollars. She told him of the unveiling in Sydney, Australia, documented in a trade magazine on September 28, 2018, after a suitable mounting had been designed for it by Musson Jewellers. "The most interesting part of the history they have posed is that it must be from the famous Indian source, the Golconda Mines, and would probably have been cut some hundred years ago. They judge this because of it's clarity and the style of the cutting. This places the diamond ready for mounting into jewelry about 130 to 140 years ago.  Close enough for the 1889 Hazelnut, don't you think?" was asked with appropriate laughter from Suz.

Ollie showing no surprise at this stunned both Suz and Walt and they waited, both staring at this unique, small man that was becoming a part of their lives and their future.

He smiled a mischievous smile that they were starting to recognize, and finally said in a whisper, "You have made some good progress and tell it well. I know all of this. You knew that but it is good to hear it all in context. Now I will tell you both what I know which is not much more than what you have already discovered."

"First is a question, I think to Walt specifically! Why is finding the pendant worth your time?" was asked demanding an honest answer.

Walt answered it in detail even adding he was unclear as to why his past employer was even asking him to do the search. That he suspected there was much more involved than just finding the diamond. Both he and Suz thought there had to be something more to have asked the director of this covert company to find the necklace. It wasn't the diamond's value that they wanted. It was about finding those who had once possessed it.

Ollie's smile had now become permanent and he said in a clear and commanding voice, "I want to join you in this. I know a few things you need know and can suggest a few others. The travel will be up to you two and I will stay in the background. You do understand that whoever wants the necklace under their control probably has something they wish to hide. I suspect this could be a dangerous trail to follow. You know that already. Are you sure you want to become part of history?"

Suz coughed, reached for Walt's hand and pulled him closer. She then surprised both Walt and Ollie by calmly asking, "Ollie, what is it you know that we don't?"

Ollie starred down at the river for over a minute, then slowly raised his gaze, still not looking at either Walt or Suz,  and said, "Nazli Sabri Pasha is where you should start."

# Chapter 25

Walt, Suz and Ollie sat in silence, staring at the river below flowing by. A blue jay settled on a branch nearby, looking their way, and next a chipmunk jumped up on the porch and it too showed interest in the three that seemed to be hypnotized by what lay before them.

Walt whispered, repeating Ollie's "Nazli Sabri Pasha," and broke the silence. The blue jay made a noisy exit and the chipmunk stood up on it's hind legs, took one more long look, and then made it's escape.

"She had quite a life over her eighty-three years. She was once thought to be the richest, most elegant woman in Egypt and at one time possessor of the largest jewelry collection in the world," Walt said this emphasizing the last part of his declaration.

Ollie smiled and Suz looked at Walt with a curious expression that was noticed by both the men.

The lengthening shadows of evening's approach had reached the porch and Suz and Walt finished the last of the wine in their glasses, stood and asked Ollie if had plans for dinner. They were going to put something together in the van and he was invited to join them. He declined with a genuine thank you and said he was going to sit where he was for a while longer and then would have some leftovers here at home.

Walt and Suz had gone only a few paces when she

turned and waved a second good evening to Ollie and he returned her wave with one of his own.

As they walked the conversation was about Nazli Sabri. Walt had spent only a few minutes online searching as the link from Prince Ibrahim's interaction with Mabel Normand had referenced him as a nephew of the Khedive of Egypt. Khedive was no longer in formal use and at this time seemed to imply King Fuad to whom Nazli was then married and was considered to be the Queen of Egypt.

Suz commented, "The largest collection of jewelry in the world. Sounds like a good place to start looking for a rather exotic pendant with a huge diamond in it's center."

Once back to the van Walt fixed some scrambled eggs sided with toast and tangerine segments. Cups of coffee and ice cream for dessert was plenty for this night and the on-line search of the life of Nazli Sabri was then underway. They sat in the van's back row captain chairs positioned so reclined they could rest their bare feet on a pillow placed on the small table.

Walt commented first. "Prince Ibrahim is referenced as her nephew and also as a second cousin once removed from he Khedive of Egypt. I have followed the available family trees of the Mohammod Ali dynasty but can't find him referenced. He was close to her and one photograph shows him at the wedding reception for her son, then King Farouk to his Queen Farida. Our Prince is off to the side, drinking from a large goblet and not paying any attention to the King and Queen. This was in 1936."

Suz had been reading through the Wikipedia reference for Nazli Sabri and was making some rather uncomplimentary comments as she read. Finally she said, "What was it with these Egyptian men. What she had to put with would never happen today. It was King Fuad's second marriage and her second, after an arranged marriage when she was twenty-four. Fuad was twenty-six years older than Nazli, saw her at an opera, proposed and two weeks later they were married."

Walt didn't say anything as he knew Suz had more to say about what she was just learning about Nazli Sabri and moments later she continued describing her early education and the two years for her and her younger sister at a boarding school in Paris after her mother's early death. Her father had essentially abandoned them at the time and after returning home she was forced into an arranged marriage to a cousin. They were totally incompatible and divorced after only eleven months. An affair with the nephew of a family friend she was staying with at the time abruptly came to an end. A few months later King Fuad saw her when attending an opera, expressed his interest, proposed and they were married on May 24, 1919.

"How could they do this to her? She was a well educated, attractive and self-confident woman. To become Queen of Egypt would have it's appeal and the unfortunate first marriage and affair could have a bearing on this quick decision. Possibly she had no choice. King Fuad was older and not really a handsome man," was posed by Suz and this time Walt answered.

"Suz, there is something you should know about the men in these families at that time. They controlled almost everything, especially their families. Through generations of violence and power, one half of one percent of the population owned seventy percent of all the productive land. All the men shared in the wealth, although only the few in the direct linage and ability could rise to control the reins of power. King Fuad at this time, aided by the over-sight of the British, made the decisions for all of Egypt. Our Prince Ibrahim was accorded funds far above any value he was to the family. His third marriage was finally with an approved wife and he then had a few minor positions in the family businesses."

Suz sat up straight and staring at Walt said, "Listen to this! 'She soon was moved to the haremlik in the Abbasiya Palace. She was under pressure to produce a son and was warned that she would be confined to the haremlik if she did not do so'."

"After the birth of their first child, a son they named Farouk, she was allowed to move into Koubbeh Palace, the official royal residence. Before Fuad's death in 1936 they would have four daughters. Farouk would become King after his father's death and she became the Queen Mother. Can you believe this? The haremlik was the home of the harem!"

# Chapter 26

Suz closed down her iPad and placed it in her lap. She was dressed in the outfit she had put on that morning, blue jeans and a cotton turtleneck top. She slid her bare foot onto his nearest to her with a gentle massaging motion. He looked up to enjoy the sight of this beautiful woman but saw tears on her cheeks and the sad expression on her face. It was not what he was expecting and even though disappointed, he understood what it was that was bothering her.

"Our Nazli was a very unhappy Queen and deservedly so. It was rumored she once attempted suicide by over dosing on aspirin. After the death of Fuad in 1936, and Farouk had become King, her life continued on an unhappy path. In 1946 she left Egypt going to the United States for treatment of a kidney ailment, or at least that was the excuse that was given to the public."

Walt had said this, repeating what he had just read in the Wikipedia biography. It was where Suz was just getting to when she closed up her iPad. She looked at him and asked that they stop for the night and go to bed. "I don't want to learn anymore of that woman's sad story right now."

Walt agreed and as Suz went back to the bedroom he read the last few paragraphs of the biography. As he started to close down his iPad a new e-mail showed up in the corner of the screen. It's message was to call Larry at this number tomorrow morning at ten eastern time. It was a new number with a New York City area code.

When Walt entered the bedroom he could see Suz was in bed, wearing a night gown and had pulled the sheet back for him to join her. "I need you to hold me until I fall asleep. You can tell me the rest of Nazli's story in the morning."

"There is more and some of it is what we may need to know about if we are going to find the pendant. Once she arrives in California her life goes from wealth and high living to a small apartment, shared with her divorced daughter Fathia, living there until she died at eighty-three in 1978," Walt told Suz this as they sought a comfortable position lying together with his arms around her. She felt so good to hold that he knew sleep for him would not come easily.

Five minutes went by and then Suz pushed back, sat up and asked, "Tell me the rest of the story. I won't get to sleep not knowing."

Walt had some understanding what could cause a woman such as Nazli to have done what she did to live that life under the control of men like Fuad and later even her own son, Farouk. Suz had already read how Fuad had only allowed her to spend one hour a day with her son from his earliest years so as not to expose him to her views of how life should be lived. She was left with bring-ing up her four daughters never challenging the roles of the males in their lives. This was all new to Suz's way of thinking and it was of course disturbing to think of anyone being treated in that manner.

Walt repeated the brief description of Nazli life in

California. That after arriving in 1946, and not returning, in 1950 her son, now King Farouk, deprived her and her daughter Fathia of their rights and titles. Nazli had wisely brought with her a sizable wardrobe and, more importantly, all of her jewelry. In 1955 she purchased, for $63,000, a 28-room mansion in Beverly Hills where she lived with her daughter, her husband and their three children. They led an active and social life until in 1975 when she was forced to sell some of the best of her jewelry collection in a Sotheby auction, including a tiara and necklace from Van Cleef and Arpels that that sold for $127,500 and $140,000, respectively. In 1976 she ended up in bankruptcy court and had to sell the remainder of her and Fathia's jewelry. She had died two years later.

Suz had listened quietly and in silence. Occasionally she shuddered slightly and Walt had felt it as she had moved closer to him. He looked at her face and marveled at what he could read in her expressions. She was living Nazli's situation as Walt described the last years of this remarkable woman's life. How different it might have been for her if she had been born in another time and place.

Again, Walt was surprised at what Suz said next. "We need to go to Los Angeles and find the box that holds what was wasn't sold at the last auction, or who it was that was the buyer of the box of miscellaneous bits and pieces of little value. If the pendant's big diamond and the several other smaller solitaires were removed the pendant should be there with the other low value pieces." There was no doubt in Suz's voice as she said this and Walt was already having similar thoughts.

# Chapter 27

Suz had at first moved onto her side toward him and he put his arm around her and pulled her close. She came to him in a comfortable position but said in a sleepy voice that tomorrow morning would be preferred by her and after a few minutes rolled over with her back to him moving to have him against her. Walt had no trouble with this as he could not think of anything that felt as good as she did at that moment. He lightly rubbed her shoulders and then let his free hand slide down over her side and rest on the curve of her hip. He could hear her breathing settle into sleep and he stayed in that position for several minutes not wanting to move.

He was thinking of what had happened over the last few days. Was it ten, or more or less, he couldn't be sure. He was sure that this was who he wanted to be with the rest of his life. He couldn't let anything happen that would harm this closeness. Larry Nichols's e-mail then came to his mind and he realized he must tell her about the telephone call tomorrow before he made it. He hadn't mentioned the previous e-mail either and knew that had to be discussed first. Then he thought maybe it should be the second thing he told her in the morning.

The next morning, after a start that had been perfect, he had looked out side. Overnight a front had come through and a dusting of snow covered all within sight. It would be gone in an hour but at the moment all was a beautiful white. The local wildlife was enjoying the morning and small tracks were on the ground and several birds were flying about. It seemed to Walt that all was good in their world as it was in his. He had the waffle iron out, plugged in and was just finishing mixing the batter when Suz came up and gave him one more hug from behind telling how good it was to be alive.

Ten minutes later as they were finishing up the second waffle Walt told Suz about the e-mails from Larry. A look of surprise and she merely asked, "What does he want and do I want to know what it is?"

"I'm not sure. The first was that he was no longer working for them directly, that they were closing up the cabin and wouldn't have any operations from there in the future. That he was in Washington, D.C. and to reply to his e-mail." Walt was glad Suz showed little interest and then he added that second e-mail had come last night with Larry's request for him to call him at ten o'clock eastern time this morning.

"That is in ten minutes Mister Wainwright! What are you going to do?" was asked with much more interest than with discussing the first contact that had been made.

Walt pulled out a small phone that Suz had never seen before and now she started to look a little more concerned. "This is one of those use once and destroy phones from my past. I have box of them I have kept here in the van. I think I should use one to make this call. It should have something to do with the search for the necklace and pendant. He already knows most of what we have done already so I am sure that is what it is about. If it has to do with anything else it will be a short conversation. Like,

Goodbye!"

Suz nodded her head okay and Walt dialed the number at exactly eight and Larry's hello was after only one ring. Walt had put the phone on speaker phone and Larry first asked if Suz was there with him.

Suz quickly answered, "I am right here!Where are you?"

"Walt, you are a most fortunate man to have Suz at your side. I am in New York, across the street from Tiffany's but have already had my breakfast," was his answer in a good natured manner and then he continued, "I am now free lancing this as I was pulled off the Hazelnut project and am on leave for the next thirty days before my next assignment. Walt, I trust you can guess why but I am looking for what happened to the big, cushion cut diamond from the pendant. Do you two have any thoughts along this line?"

Walt looked at Suz and she nodded an okay to go ahead. "Larry, Suz and I have become very close to our new friends here and these friendships are complicated by the necklace and pendant. I don't know how much you know about our last few days here but we are thinking a trip to Los Angeles is next and that the Sotheby auction of 1975 may yield some continuity to the story. Nazli's leaving Egypt and bringing her jewelry collection there in 1946 is a key. I want you to understand one thing. No harm is to come to our friends here!" Walt paused, then added, "You understand what I am saying and I trust you know what I mean by no harm. None!"

Larry didn't hesitate, "I understand. I promise you I am working alone on this now and anything I find about any Company involvement will be immediately provided to you both. You know where that will leave me at this end."

Larry paused before continuing his thoughts. "I don't think they are pursuing the necklace and pendant. I think it has something to do with the current state of affairs in the Middle East and the role Egypt may play in the Israel, Palestine and Lebanon conflicts. It appears things are going in a very bad direction and they are looking for any type of scandal that could help in negotiations between the three. Even Iran appears to be in the mix. I think finding the Hazelnut was only one possible link and it has gone cold for them at the moment."

Walt hadn't taken his eyes off Suz and could see she understood what was being said between the two of them. She showed no signs of fear but only determination.

Walt finished the call by asking Larry to use e-mail to convey a telephone number and that he would use a new phone on each call. They could use the same plus and minus protocols for dates and times. He then closed the flip-top phone ending the call.

# Chapter 28

"I need to do something to clear my mind. All this seems to be taking us further in a dangerous direction. Does playing golf help you get away from things you don't want to think about? It does for me and the course should be playable by this afternoon. Is it open on Mondays?"

Walt liked the idea of playing nine holes, especially walking, and answered Suz's questions telling her that he would call the course and find out if it was open.

Suz had another thing on her mind and was dialing the number of Gemological Services of Beverly Hills at the same time Walt was calling the golf course.

"Hello, what can I do for you today to make your life better?" was answered on the second ring and caught Suz by surprise. It was just before nine o'clock in California on a Monday morning and she wasn't really expecting an answer.

"Well, you have already made my day better by that greeting. My name is Suzanne Sussman and I am trying to find the oldest gemologist in Beverly Hills. I see on your web-page your company was founded in 1979 so maybe you know him," was Suz's equally enthusiastic reply.

The laughter was genuine and the gentleman answered, "Would ninety years old this coming Wednesday meet your needs?"

Walt was about to tell Suz the course was closed on Mondays but as he heard Suz's banter on the phone he waited to listen in on her conversation.

"I think that might work out but you don't sound the least bit over eighty."

"How does being married to the same woman for sixty-four years fit the picture. But, you know, I think I am falling in love with you. Do you have a partner in life?"

"Yes! We are about to celebrate our third anniversary, also  this Wednesday."

"He is a lucky man. It makes no difference to me, but I hope it is a man. Three years is a good start. Do you need your diamond ring appraised already. Don't want to cause any problems."

Suz was smiling and paused for a moment as here was another elderly man entering her and Walt's life, all because her recognizing Mabel Normand in a photograph on an old woman's wall just a few days ago.

There was a cough on the phone and Albert Morgan introduced himself.

"Albert Morgan, it is my pleasure to make your acquaintance. We, Walter Wainwright and I, have been together just three weeks, not years, and there is no diamond on my finger. Yet!"

There was more laughter and Suz continued, "Are you familiar with the Sotheby Auction of 1975?"

"I was there and had two pieces in the auction. I think you and Walt should make me a visit. How about coming to Beverly Hills on Wednesday and we will celebtrate our good fortunes together."

Suz looked at Walt, he nodded approval and Suz

told their new friend it was a date. She had one more question and asked Albert, "Was your father a gemologist?"

"Yes, he was, as was my grandfather. One of the best in the world of jewelry, especially diamonds. He told me all the important stories of his life and I will be able to answer all your questions."

Phone numbers were exchanged and when Albert found out they were from out of town he offered a place to stay in his home. They would not be disappointed and his wife would love to have the company.

Five minutes later Suz's phone played it's incoming call and answering found Albert Morgan on the other end. "How far are you from Jackson Hole Airport? It shows your call was from Dubois. Wyoming."

"We are about an hour and a half. It is an easy drive when the road is dry," was Suz's reply.

"Okay! Can you come out here tomorrow. My son and his wife are flying out on his company's jet and can make a stop there and pick you two up. They plan to return on Friday morning and can drop you off then or if you want to go back on Thursday there are two commercial flights to Jackson we can get you on," was Albert's engaging response.

"Tell us what time and we will be there. Is your mother and father coming, too?" was laughingly asked by Suz and Albert quickly came back, "Yes, my mother and father, and I am now totally in love with you. I will have the time for you this afternoon. See you both tomorrow," and the connection was broken.

Suz had her phone on speaker phone so Walt was in on all the banter.

"Can you believe this!" was all he could add.

# Chapter 29

Walt and Suz were at the Jackson Hole Airport at 11:30 am with thirty minutes to spare. They were both similarly dressed in blue jeans, turtle necks topped with long sleeve shirts and wearing light weight canvas walking shoes. They could enter almost any western event and be thought to be the best dressed couple in attendance. Walt was a handsome man with an athletes physical appearance. Suz made no attempt to show off the beautiful woman she was and a second look was almost always required by anyone who had looked  her way. They felt confident  about the way they looked and were ready to experience the world of private jet travel.

When they had told Ollie of Suz's conversation with Albert Morgan he insisted they take the 5 carat diamond and the necklace with them. They had carefully packed a medium size suitcase that carried a change of clothes and a more formal outfit for each of them. Walt carried a small brief case with their iPads, his phone and a small pouch that contained the necklace and the diamond. In a false bottom was his gun and two magazines of bullets that he hadn't told Suz about and that he hoped would not have to be removed from their hiding place. Suz had a shoulder bag that had her phone, wallet and a number of small personal items. Walt didn't realize she had a special bear spray container that she knew how to use with efficiency.

The Citation Latitude landed exactly on time and loading the two passengers with their suitcase took only minutes. In less than two hours they were landing at the Burbank Airport.

It had been a most enjoyable flight. Albert's son's wife, Angela, was friendly and the three of them had a good conversation on the short flight. Robert Morgan, even at sixty-three, was the co-pilot and spent most of the trip up front. The pilot was on call duty with the company and would stay in a nearby hotel for the two night layover. Robert's company manufactured high end valves for many critical uses such as in nuclear submarines and rocket engines. It was headquartered in Chicago and the jet was used a great deal to ferry executives to the many meetings needed in selling and servicing their products. Occasionally a non-business flight was made, as it was for this trip. It did seem a bit expensive in Walt's thinking but he would not complain.

A car was waiting and the four were at the humble, seven bedroom home of Albert Morgan, nestled on a hillside in Beverly Hills, California thirty minutes later.

Albert was at the door just as Robert opened it, without knocking or ringing the door bell, and the introductions were made. He had been a tall man, maybe six foot five, but now was bent with age and looked Walt directly in the eyes. It were the eyes that impressed one that this was one man that still had a lust for life. His hand shake was firm and a pleasure to shake. He took both of Suz's hands and held them gently while he told her she was just what he expected and was delighted to welcome her into his life with a friendly kiss on her offered cheek.

The party went into the house through a foray and then into a large living room where Albert's wife, Loretta was seated in a big chair. A walker was next to it and she remained seated as the introductions were made. Age could not hide what a pretty woman she still was and she had an extraordinary welcoming smile. Friendship seemed immediately available and both Suz and Walt felt comfortable with all those present.

Loretta quickly established that dinner would be at six and would be served on the veranda with a peek view of the Pacific. Dress was always casual and as they were would be just fine. Albert had moved to her side and had laid his hand on her shoulder which she covered with hers. The smiles they gave each other answered all questions about the over sixty years they had been together.

"Albert, take these new friends around the house, show them their room and you may take them to your place downstairs, but only for a quick look. Then come back up here and we can talk a bit.

The bedroom was large with it's own full bath and large closet. Big windows viewed a private and beautiful landscaped backyard. Albert asked that they drop their bags and come with him. Two doors down the hall had them enter an elevator and moments later they entered his downstairs room. The laboratory, as he referred to it.

It was an open space, maybe 30 by 40 feet was Walt's guess, and had an open office area with a big desk, office chair and three large stuffed chairs opposite. The walls had display cases with various collectible items and photographs. A number of posters advertising auctions and shows, featuring jewelry, were on the walls. Some were works of art in themselves. There were two work areas, one of which was enclosed in with viewing windows. There was a large amount of what could be assumed to be gem cutting equipment, everything clean and neat. It appeared at least a dozen could work there at the same time and not feel crowded.

Walt and Suz just stood still and stared at what was before them. Albert broke the silence saying, "There was a time I had a full staff here which most times was ten people. The neighbors, early on, were very tolerant as over the years I took in many of their children as paid apprentices. As we all aged, it became less and less and now it is only me, and one or two old time cutters that come over now and then to do a little work for themselves. We will spend a little time here tomorrow morning and you can show me why you are here. I will also explain the why."

It was then back upstairs and Walt and Suz were left in front of their bedroom door.

"Dinner is at six," was repeated by their host as he strode down the hall and disappeared around a corner.

# Chapter 30

Once in the room they looked at each other for a moment and then started to quietly laugh. Walt put his arms around Suz in a gentle hug and then kissed her.

"Right now I am thinking about seeing you being dragged over to the pile of your things behind The Hitching Rack and wondering if I should get involved with what was going on. That ugly bruiser didn't seem to be treating you right so I came to your rescue. I am now in the guest bedroom of a once major player in the international diamond market with what may be hundreds of thousands of dollars involving a necklace and pendant lifted from the collection of a past Queen of Egypt by a young Prince and given to a Hollywood silent movie star." Walt saying all this without releasing Suz and then adding, "In less than three weeks I have fallen in love with you, wanting some day to be remembering this moment sixty years from now and still being in love with you."

Suz leaned back to look into Walt's eyes. She was smiling and had never been more sure of anything in her life than the relationship she had with this man and told him, "I have no doubts about us. The rest of my life I want to be with you, be held by you and be kissed by you."

They stood together in comfortable embrace for a few minutes, both enjoying the revelations to each other and then Suz asked, "What do you think will happen tomorrow morning downstairs? Will we know what we are to do with the necklace?"

"I have no idea but it seems that Albert Morgan knows why we are here. I think he bought one of the cushion diamonds Ollie sold to Tiffany in New York some fifty, sixty years ago and sees that our contact with him goes together with the mysterious disappearance of the Hazelnut necklace. He may be able to put some of the puzzle together for us that we don't know. I am starting to think the warning to Ollie was about something that is no longer relevant."

"Wouldn't it be nice if we can find the pendant and put the necklace together again. Someone has the 25.09 carat diamond. I hope it wasn't cut up into smaller ones. I want to see it all together. Would be a pretty expensive bauble for me to wear around the van in the Dubois Campground, don't you think?" was Suz's comment as she teased Walt's hair.

Dinner was the six of them. Drinks were offered but all chose the dinner wine selected by Albert, a nice Cabernet. A tenderloin steak, baked potato and broccoli were presented on each plate and was excellent, as was the conversation. Some personal and some general interest but none about diamonds or jewelry.

It became more obvious to Walt and Suz that Loretta was in early stages of dementia and she was made to feel a part of the conversation by all those at the table. Some of her personal stories of their family were most interesting to Walt and Suz and enthusiastically received by the others, although they had surely heard them before. It made the two newcomers understand what good people they were with and left no doubts about trusting them.

Dessert of small scoops of vanilla ice cream, topped with chocolate syrup and a large raspberry was just right with good coffee to finish a most delightful evening. To add to it Robert asked Walt and Suz if they would like to stay over the next day and play nine, or eighteen holes, at the Los Angeles Golf Club that afternoon. They mentioned they didn't have their clubs with them, as Robert already knew, and he smiled telling them that after lunch tomorrow he would take them down to Albert's golf room and they would be outfitted.

The good nights were said, with hugs from Loretta and hand shakes with Albert.

Walt and Suz were in their room by nine o'clock and could only smile at each other. They readied for bed and Suz came out from the bathroom dressed in her short night gown giving Walt the smile he was beginning to like seeing and in a few minutes they were enjoying what this evening had brought them even more.

Sleep was not going to come easily as life was much too good right then to spend this time sleeping.

"How much fun I am having. Never, even in my wildest dreams, can this be happening. Tomorrow morning could change our lives. And I think in a good way," was Suz's first words after they had got settled laying together just touching.

Walt was not quite so sure about the good way it would turn out but he was in such satisfied state that nothing could take that feeling away at the moment. Words weren't necessary and they soon got into their sleeping positions, with Suz on her side and Walt laying against her back with his arm around her waist.

# Chapter 31

Walt and Suz woke early and enjoyed being able to have a few hours to start the  new day. They dressed in what they would want for golf. Suz in three quarter length shorts and collared golf shirt and Walt in light weight slacks and also a collard golf shirt. They would wear their canvas walking shoes. They made a nice looking couple and would be welcomed at even the most prestigious of golf clubs.

In the dinning room was a side board with dry cereal choices, fruit and everything needed to fix breakfast. On the table was a note from Robert telling them the tee time was at two o'clock and they would meet here for a light lunch and leave in time to have at least fifteen minutes to hit a few practice balls and do some putting.

Also, that Albert was downstairs and they should go down as soon as they had finished breakfast. He would take them to the golf room after they concluded what ever business it was with Albert was finished. "You will have a great morning with Albert and be able to share in his very special world," was added at the bottom of the note.

As they descended in the elevator they both could not contain their excitement. Walt had the 5 carat diamond and the empty necklace in his pocket. Albert was at his big desk and waved them into his space. Rachmaninoff Number two was, at low volume, in the background. There was a square, blue cloth pad on the desk and Albert's first words were, "Why don't you show me what you have brought for me to look at."

Walt pulled the small packet out of his pocket and let the diamond fall onto the middle of the pad. Albert said, "Ahhh," and picked it up in his fingers. He then turned on the desk light and placed the stone in a special tweezers. He positioned his loupe and started a careful examination. He then said, "Hmmm," and placed the diamond on a scale and mumbled, "Five point one is close enough."

"Will you show me the necklace now, or tease me a little longer?" Albert had a sly smile on his face as he said this, leaning forward in anticipation. He wasn't disappointed as Walt reached into his pocket and pulled out the felt draw string bag that held it. He placed it on the desk but not such that Albert could easily reach it.

"How about you tell us the story of why we are here and why you knew what it was that we would bring with us. You know a part of the missing Tiffany Hazelnut necklace story and we may be able to tell you a good deal more." was said by Walt such that Albert knew he would have to share what he knew.

Albert leaned back in his chair and a wide grin lit up his face. "You two are such neat people. So nice to have as guests, and hopefully for friends. I will start with that my grandfather, and later my father, were employed by Tiffany, New York, when I was born. My grandfather had immigrated from England and had done his apprenticeship there. He and a friend had come over together and were witnesses to the build up of the Hazelnut necklace. My grandfather built a lot of the four leaf diamond clusters that tie the solitaire diamond settings together. He spent hours and hours working on this and always thought it the highlight of his career in jewelry. He told the stories to me over and over as he taught me what I know. Sometime in the late 1920's a man showed up at Tiffany with two, 2 carat diamonds to sell. It was my father that evaluated them and the diamond buyer made the offer. All that was known about the seller was that he called himself John Smith, wanted cash and no paperwork. My father said he was nice in appearance and manner and the deal was made. The diamonds were nearly perfect in clarity and judged very fine stones. The cut was old style as it is described now. A nice cut but could have been better if done twenty years later."

"My father told me that at the time he thought he had seen these diamonds before and that they were very much like the ones they had placed in the Hazelnut necklace. John Smith returned to sell a single diamond several more times over the years, always the same quality but in increasing sizes. My father started to collect these using up almost all his savings, much to my mother's disgust. A dealer in Chicago contacted him about buying several diamonds from a John Smith over the years and my father bought those. When my father retired I bought out his collection."

Albert smiled as he watched his two guests as he pulled a small pouch from his desk drawer and dropped two, cushion shaped diamonds on the pad. Both Walt and Suz recognized them immediately as the ones that sided the central diamond they had just placed in front of Albert. "These came to us later, maybe 1962. One through Tiffany and another to me more indirectly from an old collector in

Chicago. I purchased the diamonds as my father had told me the story of the Hazelnut necklace many times and I wanted to put it back together again. This started  my life long search for the necklace itself."

Walt opened the pouch and let the necklace slide out onto the pad. Albert sat absolutely still for several minutes, staring at what had just been put in front of him, before saying in a reverent voice, "I have waited sixty years to see this, not knowing if it even existed anymore. Just in time one of my most important dreams has come true. I can't tell you how much this means to me. If you don't mind I would like to place all the diamonds so we can see the necklace as it was when shown in 1889 at the Paris Exposition for the first time. The pendant is also a story I can tell you about and it is in my safe over there," he said pointing to the big safe built into the opposite wall.

"It was in a boxed lot of bits and pieces at the 1975 Fine Jewelry auction put on by Sotheby Parke Bernet here in Los Angeles. I bid the winning bid on it on a whim and it was in the bottom of the box covered by low value pieces. All the diamonds had been removed but I still knew what is was when I first saw it."

As Albert told them this he thought that maybe he should have told them the real story but he had given his word not to and would live with that. Later he had added a cluster of five diamonds to replace the missing Hazelnut diamond and replaced all the smaller ones. He could now present the complete Hazelnut necklace and pendant even though the big namesake diamond had been substituted for. He tried to hide his smile and waited.

Suz looked at Walt and he suggested she tell their story. She did and Albert was mesmerized by the tale of

Prince Ibrahim and Mabel Normand. The pendant re-moved from the necklace with them headed out into the Paris night to party with the necklace worn by Mabel and the pendant stuffed into the Prince's pocket. The story of Mabel's death and before that the reason for her giving the necklace to the Smiths to support the adoption of a baby born to a befriended, unwed mother who had died at childbirth.

As Suz had told the part of Mary White, raised, married, widowed and still living in Dubois, Wyoming, Albert had let a tear run down his cheek. He wiped it away with no embarrassment and said, "That is such a good story. Good people with a good story. How rare in today's world."

"It is time to go to the golf room and get you outfitted. I will work on the necklace and we can find time to discuss how to proceed with our little project later this afternoon. Finding the 25.09 carat Hazelnut diamond is the last major hurdle to clear."

# Chapter 32

The golf room looked more like a golf store. There were six golf bags filled with sets of clubs, probably twenty putters on a rack ready to be picked through and a putting mat to try them out on. A full size practice station with net and mat took up one end of the room. On one wall was a display of a collection of antique wood shafted clubs, some very old and looked to be quite valuable.

"Pick out which set of clubs you think will work and set them by the door. When you are ready to go after lunch Robert will come down with you and show you the way out to the car. You are only ten minutes to the club's parking lot. Have a fun day and I will have a surprise for you when you get back."

Suz had no problem picking out her bag as a set of three year old TaylorMades were there, men's right hand with regular shafts, exactly the same as her own clubs. Walt found a set of Callaways with stiff shafts that felt right in his hands. He stepped over the practice mat and dragged a ball over. A seven iron had been picked and it took only one swing to tell him he had his clubs for this day. Each bag contained a dozen new Titleist ProV1 golf balls. On a table was box of used once golf gloves and they each picked out two. They were ready and at that moment Robert came into the room and announced lunch was being served.

Sandwich makings were on the side board and were quickly assembled. Albert came in with Loretta and he made sandwiches for them both and loaded the plates with chips and  pickles. It was almost like a picnic as they took their seats around the table.

Suz sat down next to Loretta and she reached for her arm telling her, "Albert is so excited about finding his Hazelnut necklace. Just last week he mentioned it again. About never finding it or what had happened to it. His grandfather helped build it and he also wanted to know where it was, but never did. He passed on not knowing. So did his father. Look at him! So happy he looks like a little boy again with a new toy. Thank you two for being here and making this happen."

Suz gave Loretta's hand a firm squeeze and whispered as if it was a secret, "He is a very nice man. It has been a good life for you, hasn't it?" Loretta looked at Suz with some moister coming to her eyes and said in calm and loving way, "You will never know how good a man he is, and has been. My life could have been no better. But enough of this. You have to concentrate on your golf game and beat them soundly today to keep them in their place. I wish Albert could still play. He was a good player and loved the game."

They drove into the Los Angeles Country Club at 1:15 and two golf carts were at the car before Robert could stop the engine. He popped the trunk lid and the four bags were on the right carts by the time they managed to get to them. "Have a good round," chorused the two attendants at the same time Robert handed each a five dollar bill.

Robert guided Walt and Suz to the cart area next to

the first tee, parked behind several others lined up, and the starter said their two o'clock was on time. Robert and Angela went into the clubhouse while Walt and Suz chose to do a little putting to get used to the greens. Walt started watching Suz as she had a beautiful stroke and the ball seemed to roll smoothly to the hole with just the right pace.

At the first tee there was a gallery of mostly men that had come out from the clubhouse bar. The two ladies decided to play the same "bell" tees as the men. The first hole, a par 5, stretches 548 yards with just a slight leftward bend and Suz was given the honors. No one there had ever seen her swing a club. A gasp came from all, including Walt, as they watched an almost perfect swing by a beautiful woman that had the ball tracing the ideal path into the middle of the fairway.

The day was so good on the course that Walt knew they would be playing a lot of golf together as long as they were able. Angela was also a good player with a fifteen handicap. Robert was a very respectable twelve. Walt was a good player and at one time played at a single digit. His first shot of the day had him next to Suz's ball and it would continue that way through the nine holes they played.

It was on the 200 yard third hole that they had a moment of real excitement. Suz, still with the honors hit her three wood perfectly, landing the ball just short of the green between the two sand traps, and they all watched as it rolled up to the pin, stopping just five inches from making a hole in one.

The last hole for them was Number 9, a 187 yard par three, hitting over a wash and to a green protected by three big sand traps, one in front and the other two on either side. After the tee shots there were  four balls in the sand. A small gallery had formed around the green as the word of the two good looking women playing good golf had spread through the afternoon bar attendees. Walt was away and hit out a respectable shot twenty-five feet below the pin. Angela match his shot, but five feet closer to the hole. Robert in the left trap had a more difficult shot but hit a good one that almost hit Angela's ball before it stopped rolling ten feet passed. Suz had the most difficult shot from the left side trap and making a perfect swing had her ball roll up to the pin, hit it and then coming to a stop three feet away. The gallery erupted in applause and she had two proposals for marriage as they finished their game. The foursome was invited back to the clubhouse for drinks but demurred with good grace.

It had been a nice nine holes and played in just over two hours. Each had had the good experience of becoming familiar of the character of each other that the game of golf so often provides. Both Walt and Suz were feeling Robert and Angela could become friends and they, in turn, came away with same impression of Walt and Suz. For Walt it was how good a golfer Suz was and how they worked together to make the game a pleasure. He had no doubt that his future was tied to this remarkable woman.

# Chapter 33

The foursome was back to Albert's by 4:45 and went in through the outside doorway to the golf room. Walt and Suz carried their golf bags and once inside placed them where they had been found. The barely used golf gloves went back in the box and since they hadn't lost any balls they had left the two used balls with the still new ten ones in each bag.

It had been a great outing and all four were busy commenting how much they had enjoyed playing together. Going into the hall they could see into Albert's room well enough to notice the two bottles of wine and six glasses placed on the big work bench. The elevator door opened and Albert wheeled Loretta in, asking all to come with him into the shop as he had something to show them.

Loretta was beaming, her eyes were clear and there was no doubt that she knew what was going to be shown to them. She said as an announcement, "Albert has been down here all afternoon working. Robert, would you pour our wine. We can toast Albert and then he will show us something very special."

Robert poured and Angela served. Albert had them line up on the opposite side of the bench from where he was standing and asked Loretta be positioned between the two girls. The boys were to be the bookends. The room was in semi-darkness and Albert reached under the table and pulled out a two foot square, two inch thick, dark blue velvet covered board that had a raised object on it covered by a matching blue velvet drape. The smile he had made him look twenty years younger and Loretta seemed the same, young again.

Albert bent down and flipped a switch. Under a spot light the blue velvet glistened and the room seemed to have become even darker. Loretta couldn't hold her enthusiasm and told Albert, "Hurry up and let us see what you have done this time!"

Albert lifted the dark cloth away and the Hazelnut necklace, with it's pendant, glistened under the spot light. Refracted rays of bright light scattering about the room seeming to light up the entire space.  It was presented on a dark blue velvet covered pedestal shaped in the form of a woman's neck, shoulders and with the curves of breasts, all in perfect proportion.

Suz reached for Loretta, putting her arm around her, and saying, "It is so beautiful. I have never seen anything like it before. In magazines maybe, but never in person. Albert, you put this all together this afternoon? Albert, it is gorgeous!"

The toasts were made, Albert was embarrassed by all the compliments and kept insisting he had only re-assembled the jewelry his grandfather had helped create. When the wine bottles and glasses were empty it was time to go upstairs and ready for dinner at seven.

Albert ask Suz and Walt to remain with him for a few minutes. He picked up the necklace, with it's pendant, and asked Suz if she would like to try it on. She chose to just hold it for a minute, and then handed it back to him. Albert went over to his big safe, opened the door and asked his two new partners to take a look inside. Among it's varied contents there were a number of identical metal storage drawers. He pulled one out and set it on the bench.

"I am showing you something I want you never to talk about to anyone else. I really mean this. To no one! Robert knows about the safe, has the combination and is the executor of my will. He can guess, but doesn't really have an idea what is in these drawers."

He had placed the drawer under a flood light and opened the lid so that Walt and Suz could look directly down into it's contents. In small felt lined boxes were hundreds of diamonds. The diamonds sparkled and cast their rays in all directions in a mesmerizing manner.

"These are one carat round cut in various grades but all good enough to be mounted in high quality settings. Pretty, aren't they?" was asked as he closed the lid, placing the drawer back in the safe and taking out another, similar one. "These are two carat rounds. You can see not so many but still a nice collection." In one of the boxes were several rings with solitaire diamonds and he picked one out and looked at Suz and asked her, "Would you like to try it on your ring finger, left hand of course."

Suz blushed, looked to Walt for approval, and held out her hand. The ring fitted perfectly, positioning itself with the diamond sparkling under the overhead lights. Suz wasn't sure what to do at first as she was sure something was going on between the three of them she didn't understand. She took one last admiring look at the ring, slipped it off and  handed it back to Albert.

He accepted it, held it up to the light for one last look and then handed it to Walt saying, "This is for you for when the time is right. Don't wait too long."

# Chapter 34

They had a half hour to get ready for dinner and both Walt and Suz wanted to shower. Suz suggested that Walt go first as she had a few things she needed to think about. It had been a big day of new experiences and Albert had put something on the table at the last minute that now had her own future to think about.

Walt was facing the shower head with the strong stream beating on his face and shoulders. It felt good as he mulled over what had happened just a few minutes ago. He had no doubts any more and had made his decision about his future with Suz. It had to be with her and he was going to ask her to join him. The next thing he felt was her arms around his waist, her hands holding him against her.

They dried each off and before dressing he retrieved the ring from his pants pocket and showed it to her. "If you are ready I want you to be my wife. Married or not, I want you with me the rest of my life. The ring is a symbol and if at any time you change your mind all you have to do is take it off your finger. It is yours to keep."

Suz was silent for enough time that Walt started to think he had misjudged their relationship but then she smiled and putting her arms around his neck told him, "I was thinking while you were in the shower how to answer your question if you asked, or if I would have to tell you how ready I am to say yes, even if you didn't."

They were ten minutes late to dinner and the four waiting for them had no doubt of the why of their tardiness. Loretta merely said in casual manner, "What a pretty ring Suz. It looks like it has found a nice place on your hand. What does Walt think of all this?"

Albert was watching intently as he was witnessing a change in Loretta these last two days. Her eyes seemed to be clearer and she was paying attention to what was going on around her, even initiating conversations. He knew there was no evidence to support much recovery from early signs of dementia once it had begun. In any case the mere sight of her showing the interest in Suz and Walt brought some happiness that had been missing in his life for many months. He also had this new challenge to share with this young couple. That of finding the Hazelnut diamond, or at least find out what had happened to it.

Robert and Angela both noticed Loretta's change in demeanor but would keep it to it themselves as neither realized her seeming recent withdrawal might be early dementia. It did make Robert think that maybe it was time for him to hand over the everyday management of his company to others and spend more time with Angela, and with Albert and Loretta before it was too late.

Dinner was served with an excellent lasagna from a small, local delicatessen and sided with salad and fresh baked Italian bread completing the menu. Red wine was served and all were satisfied. For dessert were choices of gelato ice cream and a selection of special biscotti. With coffee to finish the meal the conversation turned to what might be next. All were interested and Albert led the discussion. First he asked Walt and Suz if they were comfortable with him keeping the necklace in his safe while they started the search for the Hazelnut diamond. That they should just refer to it as  Hazel. Next he posed that he would make out a personal check to Oliver Bennett for the necklace and the 5 carat round diamond that Walt and Suz had brought with them. Ollie was to keep the check until the team had run the hunt to it's end, and if not successful, cash it as payment in full. He suggested Ollie should wait until the search concluded and that he join the group if he wished. It was Albert's thought that if the diamond was found, or a suitable one to replace it, the Hazelnut necklace would become many times more valuable and the share for each of them would far exceed what was now offered to him.

That was the agreement decided upon and hands were shaken and kisses on cheeks made. Robert's plane would pick them at Burbank Airport at 9:30 in the morning and would land in Jackson Hole in time to let Walt and Suz be able to drive to Dubois before dark.

The search for Hazel was getting serious. Albert then gave Walt and Suz a small pouch which contained a ring having eight mounting prongs of a rather irregular round shape that could hold a large, cushion cut diamond. It had been made from a drawing, in his grandfather's hand, as a possible mount for the 25.09 carat diamond that was instead placed in the Hazelnut Necklace pendant and displayed at the 1889 Paris Exposition. Two rings had been made and the other one was missing.

Both Walt and Suz thought that they had seen a ring similar to this one before.

# Chapter 35

The next morning breakfast was taken care of and the good byes and thank yous expressed. Suz had a special hug with Loretta and promised that she and Walt would be back soon to spend more time with her and Albert. Albert had taken Walt aside and told him he didn't realize how quickly he would give Suz the ring but in cases like this, soon could sometimes not be soon enough.

The plane was on the runway apron, with the engines running, when they arrived at 9:30. Loading was accomplished quickly and with a clear runway the tower instructed them clearance to take off. Twenty minutes later Los Angeles was disappearing behind them. At 2:00 pm they were driving into Dubois and minutes later entering the van. Suz happily said, "Home, sweet home." She turned to Walt and accepted his embrace and  gentle kiss.

They stood together this way for a long moment, then Suz kissed Walt, leaned back looking into his eyes. "I am happy, Walter Wainwright. I can't ever remember feeling this way before. Not sure happy is the right word but I don't want to be anywhere else or be with anyone else. Right here with you is what I want more than anything I can think of."

"I feel the same and happiness is the right word. The real meaning of the word. One needs to treasure such a feeling as it is so seldom experienced. Some wise man once said that the achievement of happiness should be the goal of ones life. For us it is being together that makes it possible. I never want to loose it so you will have to be with me the rest of my life."

Suz wiped a tear away, kissed him once more and then asked if they should try to meet with Ollie before it got dark outside. Walt agreed, but wanted a few more minutes holding her before he was ready to leave the van.

As they approached Ollie's house they could see him sitting on the table, feet on the bench facing the river, but this time his posture was upright and when he heard them approach he turned and greeted them with clear eyes and a big smile.

A bottle of no label wine was uncorked and glasses filled. Walt and Suz traded telling of their meeting with Albert Morgan and Loretta. Of the luxury of flying private jet and about Robert and Angela. Then Walt handed Ollie the small envelope containing the hundred thousand dollar check.

Ollie opened the envelope, slid the check out far enough to see the amount and then slid it back placing the envelope in his jacket pocket. "Now tell me about the necklace," was his unconcerned comment.

They did, again trading turns, and it took a full glass of wine to finish describing the three days. Suz described the unveiling of the filled in necklace and pendant under the spot light and how beautiful it looked.

"And the ring on your finger?" Ollie asking this as he took Suz's left hand in his, holding it up to make a close, appreciative examination. Walt told of Albert showing them a collection of diamonds and picking the ring out of a small box containing several others, and placing it on

Suz's ring finger. About her admiring it, then giving it back and his response of handing it to him telling him not wait too long. Less than two hours later it was on Suz's finger and they planned to have it stay there the rest of their lives. Ollie raised his glass, nodded toward them, and they touched glasses with a nice clink. "Excellent!" was Ollie's only comment.

The conversation then turned back to the Hazelnut necklace. Ollie started by pointing out that 1875 was a busy year as on November 16 of that year Joseph Halpern and Company declared bankruptcy, owing $3,000,000 to creditors. That he must have sold the 25.09 carat diamond to Tiffany before then. Therefore they could assume it was in Tiffany's possession from then until some time after the 1889 Paris Exposition.

"It was only fourteen years before then, in 1861, that we have any idea of it's movement, which is interesting in itself but of not much use. Halpern had first sold it to Abdul Aziz, a Turkish sultan, who reigned from June, 1861 until deposed May 30, 1876. It was reported he had died six days later under mysterious circumstances. He had given the diamond as a wedding present to someone in the family of Isma'il Pasha, the Khedive of Egypt and ruler of Sudan at the time. He only reined until 1879 after driving his country into bankruptcy. It can be surmised that he sold it to Halpern and he, in turn, had sold it to Tiffany before his 1875 bankruptcy, as mentioned as falling on hard times in the Tiffany Diamond photograph's side bar."

Ollie paused for a moment and then with a sly smile on his face added, "After Tiffany's causal remark of it's disappearance, and the possibility of its diamonds being reset in other jewelry, that should be your starting point."

Walt was quick to answer Ollie with, "You do understand that it must be our starting point. You are going to go along for the ride with us, aren't you?"

Ollie smiled at them and answered, "I think that is something I would like to do. I will let you do the travel and the dirty work and I will work from here. Maybe not just on the picnic table but occasionally even from my home office."

# Chapter 36

It was decided to have dinner in town and Ollie called Mary to see if she and Alice could join the group. Next was an invite to Jack to the party, they all would meet at The Lone Buffalo Steakhouse and the time would be early. Six o'clock, in forty five minutes. Ollie made the table reservation and by sixty-thirty the orders had been placed. The evening went well, the food was good and the conversations were even better. The diamond search was only mentioned a few times and by eight the good nights were being said, smiles and hugs exchanged and the happy group split up and went their separate ways,

Walt, Suz and Jack walked back to the campground together and said their good nights there. Once in the van Walt and Suz were both wide awake and after a few moments spent with a hug and kiss they decided to spend some time on their iPads.

They were both busy for about a half hour when Suz poked Walt and told him that she had turned over her business management to her top team member for the next six months. Chasing Hazel would be too disrupting for her to co-ordinate the finding and rescuing of lost young people.

Walt smiled at this. He knew exactly why Suz needed this break. Some searches came easily and rescues simple. Others faced a myriad of difficulties and required full attention with no outside distractions. He leaned over to say, "That's a good decision. Making mistakes are too costly for all involved. Chasing Hazel has a few risks, I suppose, but there is no rush and I don't think there is any problem if we aren't successful."

Suz looked at Walt as he said this and then started to laugh. "So neither of us has any income and we are getting ready to search the world for a lost diamond the size of a big hazel nut. How is that for the future of a newly engaged couple?" As she said this she got up from her chair and straddled Walt sitting on his lap. It was decided that all else could wait until tomorrow.

It wasn't to be as just at the wrong moment Walt's phone rang it's familiar melody. Looks exchanged, he reached over and answered the call as it showed it was Albert Morgan

"Hello Albert! Have something for us?" was asked in as neutral a voice as Walt could summon. The answer was, "Is Suz close by? This is for you both."

Walt covered the phone and Suz, barely able to refrain from laughing out loud, managed to call out, "I am here and Walt will put us on the speaker phone. What have you discovered. Not Hazel in one of your bins?"

Albert knew, or at least hoped he knew, what he had just interrupted but continued, "I have been able to contact an old friend that was an apprentice with me at Tiffany. I wasn't sure he was still living but a search on this on-line thing found him in just a couple of minutes. He his living with his son in, get this, Castle Pines, Colorado. He would like to have you make a visit. He remembers many of his grandfather's stories about working on the Hazelnut and remembered my grandfather, and father.

We had a good conversation and he wants you to come down for a visit. Let me give you his telephone number and maybe you and Suz could set up a date to meet. By the way his son's place is on the golf course there. Yes, that one!"

Before Albert could continue Walt interrupted, "Albert, I want to use another phone for this so give me a couple of minutes and I will call you back. You won't recognize the phone number. Just say hello." He broke the connection and had Suz move enough for him to get up to get to one of the cabin drawers and retrieve one of his untraceable flip phones. He dialed Albert's number and it was answered after two rings.

"I won't ask what is going on but here's the number. Call them tomorrow and then call me back around noon my time." Albert sounded excited by this and repeated the number, the name Lenard Potash and the son's, Nick. Then said goodbye and the connection was broken.

Suz looked at Walt and couldn't hide the concern she was feeling about this cloak and dagger stuff involving someone like Albert. She waited and it was difficult for Walt to answer the obvious question she had.

"I am out of what I was in before and I have no interest in getting anyway involved in it ever again. The two contacts we have had with Larry is suspicious but I don't think are a threat. I can't be certain but there is a chance my old employer is still monitoring my telephone. They don't record conversations, unless something is top secret at their end. Just numbers called and cross referenced. If it is not in the data base it's record is deleted."

Suz looked even more concerned. "I knew this would happen and should have been ready for it. But not with Albert. We are all involved now, aren't we. Mary, Ollie, Jack, Albert, his old friend Lenard Potash, and me," was said in a shaky voice.

Walt pulled her close and told her not to worry as what ever was going on he didn't think anyone in the Company would have any interest in what they were doing. That more likely it was Larry that was using what connections he still had to try to find out what their group was learning in their search for Hazel. "My guess there is some way to monetize the finding of Hazel, not the diamond, but by it's connection to others."

Suz was still concerned but pulled Walt over to her and told him, "Tomorrow morning we will continue our search. Wake me up if I am still asleep and we will finish what we had just started before Albert called. I'll bet he knew the minute you answered the phone what was going on. Your voice changes. Did you know that?"

# Chapter 37

Walt had waited until eleven o'clock the next morning to call Lenard Potash. It was his son that answered the phone and an immediate conversation was how good it had been to listen in on the conversation his father had with Albert. That he hadn't seen that kind of happiness in his father for several years. All his old friends had passed on and the rekindling of an old friendship was important for him. Especially now as he knew his life was nearing it's end.

The plans were made quickly and all Walt and Suz had to do was get there and bring their golf clubs. The chase of Hazel seemed almost enchanted as it gathered this group together in a most enjoyable manner. Meeting more like Albert Morgan, his family, and now Lenard Potash and his son. Adding to this was private jet flights and golf outings. Castle Pines golf course was a top ten in any golfer's want to play list.

They would drive down in the morning. It was close to four hundred and fifty miles but mostly on the Interstate. Seven hours possible driving time but Walt figured a little over eight as he wanted to run the Wagoneer through a car wash when they got close. Clean it looked much better. At the town home development they had a guest cottage and it was reserved for them for two nights. They had an afternoon tee time the next day for the three of them and Nick was sure he could get the club pro to play at least nine holes with them.

Walt looked at Suz while he talked to Nick and she sat with an expression of sheer wonder on how these new relationships were happening for them. A shadow seemed to fall over her face as she thought, "This is just too good to be true."

Walt could read the look on her face and he said, "It is too good to be true, don't you think? It's not! What we are entering is into the lives of the greatest generation. Have you read Tom Brokaw's book? Actually, maybe it was the generation before that was the greatest and these are the children they raised. In any case, let's go down to our bench and watch the river go by. I will call Albert from there."

The river did it's magic as the two sat close together, watching the water swirl and eddy around the rocks and stones in the river bed. Then Walt made the call to Albert.

He was excited that Walt had made contact with the Potash's so quickly. "Len and I started our apprenticeships about the same time. Both our fathers were among the best of the gemologists at Tiffany at the time and so we had some privilege but we loved the work and were good at doing it. This didn't get in the way of having a good time, both at work and in our free time. Len is a short man and as you know I am tall. We took a good deal of teasing when we went out on the town together. It was a good time."

Albert paused for what seemed to Walt and Suz to be a bit long, then he continued, "We both married, after about ten years of playing the field, myself to Loretta and

Len to a delightful young and pretty woman who passed away much too soon. We each had but one child, Robert for me and Nick for Len, who you will meet tomorrow."

Again he paused. This time they could hear his breathing was coming hard for him. He coughed and then continued, "I left Tiffany and came out to California as a independent gemologist and Len stayed in New York with Tiffany until he retired. I never made contact with him, or he with me, until I searched for him on-line yesterday. I was surprised that he was still alive as he had always had medical issues as a young man. It was good to hear his voice again and we are planning to meet up and talk old times soon. It has to be soon, you do understand."

This was followed by some pleasantries and wishing Walt and Suz success in the hunt for Hazel and if they had the chance to play Castle Pines be sure to do it.

Walt and Suz decided that evening to fix a chicken salad and with a half of a baguette and bottle of wine they returned to the picnic table to have dinner and watch the river run by. There was a sadness with them following their talk with Albert that was bothering them both. Suz broached the subject first. "Something happened between them, maybe sixty years ago, that caused a friendship to dissolve like that. Just Albert going out to California wouldn't have broken it up like that."

They were on the road early the next morning. It was a nice Fall day, the traffic light and the Wagoneer was actually a nice vehicle to drive.

What had occurred in the conversation with Albert was still on their minds and neither wanted to speculate on what they were thinking about this friendship that had suddenly ended those many years ago. Suz tried to find something on the radio without success. NPR came in and out as the weak signals didn't do well in the mountainous terrain. As the radio started to receive the Laramie signal the biased coverage of the over a year in advance of the 2024 election pushing the sad figure of Joe Biden in censored coverage versus the dismissal of anything positive of the probable Donald Trump candidate made it hard to listen to.

"I made a mistake in the last election. I voted against Trump and for Biden. What a mess he has made of everything he has touched. You can understand why the only things the liberals talk about are his executive orders spending money we don't have. Everything he has done is going terribly wrong." As Suz said this Walt hit the off button and they drove in silence for the next half hour.

It was time for lunch and a picnic spot showed up just in time. Walt had taken Highway 287 highway south and they were in the mountainous part which provided some good scenery as well as a blue sky and comfortable temperature. They could forget the rest of the world for a bit and enjoy the sandwiches Suz had made for the trip.

Walt suddenly stood saying, "Look up there! On the ridge just to the left of the stand of trees. Three, maybe four, big horn sheep. It is our lucky day!"

# Chapter 38

They arrived at the outskirts of Denver just as an increase in traffic was forming. Passing Mile High Stadium they were soon back up to the speed limit for the next half hour that had them exiting at Happy Canyon Road. A few minutes later they were at the Castle Pines entrance. The young man at the gate house, upon hearing they were the guests of Nick Potash, handed them a map he had left at the gate for them, gave them verbal instructions on how to reach Ridge Plaza Drive and an enthusiastic wish for them to have a nice visit.

They were parking outside the address they had been given when a tall, handsome man in his early sixties came out to great them. He opened the door for Suz to exit the Wagoneer with a warm welcome and introduced himself as Nick Potash. He then turned to Walt with a like welcome and handshake. It was then inside the town home to meet the very short and elderly Len Potash. His bright blue eyes, big smile and greeting had Walt and Suz immediately feeling very good about this visit.

The formalities having been taken care of Nick suggested they take some wine out to the porch that had a nice view looking out over the golf course where it could be seen through the numerous big pine trees. The chairs were comfortable and the chilled white wine excellent. A plate of substantial hors d'oeuvres sat within easy reach.

Len was excited to have heard from his long lost friend and said how they should have made contact long ago. Walt and Suz could sense that he wanted to leave the conversation at that and Walt decided to cut to the chase.

"We, with Albert, are trying to find out what happened to Tiffany's Hazelnut necklace pendant's 25.09 carat diamond. You don't have it, do you?" Walt asked with the good humor that was intended.

Len almost dropped his wine glass and choked out, "So that's what is going on here with Albert. Our grandfathers built that necklace! It was their first project with Tiffany, not the designing but making up the parts and the molds to cast them. My grandfather always said it was the most fun he ever had in his forty years at Tiffany and that Albert's grandfather was the best friend he had ever had. Albert was the best friend I ever had."

This last sentence was said in a sad manner and the glance he gave Nick was not missed by either Walt or Suz. The pause in the conversation hung over the table for a few moments and then Len repeated, "The Hazelnut necklace!" and another break in the conversation as he seemed to be gathering his thoughts.

"Our grandfathers, Albert's and mine, immigrated from England as young men. They had been raised in the area of Hatton Gardens, a section of London that was a place of creative work, however mostly known for the diamond business. The import of raw diamonds from Africa, cutting of the stones, the selling of finished diamonds and of diamond jewelry. If you were a boy there you were apprenticed early, many times just having made it through grammar school. They had done their apprenticeship with an old Jew in his small house laboratory and had shown the skills needed to become premier cutters. It was he that said to go to the land of opportunity and it was he who had a contact with Tiffany in New York"

Again Len paused, then continued describing how they had arrived in New York in 1870, just before Tiffany moved to their 15 Union Square location which became known as the Palace of Jewels. Charles Lewis Tiffany had convinced his partner, John Young, to move the company in that direction. The grandfathers had worked on the jewels, both as cutters, making mountings and building the jewels as designed to be shown at the 1879 Paris exposition. They were in position to build the Hazelnut necklace for the 1889 Exposition and had done so.

"Albert told me he has it in his safe. The complete necklace with the pendant. I knew he had found the pendant. He didn't tell me but I am still in the loop as far as what is happening in the big time jewelry market. How did you find the necklace? It was thought to be lost forever!" Len was looking at Walt as he asked this, as was Suz and Nick who was now curious about this interest in a necklace over one hundred years old.

Walt told Len, and Nick, the story of meeting Mary White in Dubois, Wyoming, of Suz recognizing Mabel Normand in the photographs on her wall and her relationship to Mary's mother and father. The use of the necklace gifted to Mabel by Prince Mohammad Ali Ibrahim in 1922 that she in turn had given it to the Smiths to support their adopted young child by the selling of it's diamonds.

Len had listened carefully and then said that in the morning he would show them his small workshop where he still cut and polished small raw diamonds. He wished them good evening as he was tired and needed his rest.

# Chapter 39

Nick rode with Walt and Suz to the guest unit and would walk back to his place. With the key he opened it up and gave them a quick tour. They were to come back to the house and have breakfast with them at eight and Len would then give them a tour of his shop. He was sure they would find it quite interesting as Len loved to show the techniques involved in producing a brilliant diamond from a little piece of odd looking, glassy pebble. It would be worth their time and it was very important for him to show off his skills, especially now. It had been his whole life and he was now thinking it was about to come to it's end. They had a tee time at 11:47.

The good nights and thank yous were given and accepted. It had been a long day, the guest unit was very nice and the big bed looked most inviting.

Minutes later Walt's phone chirped it's incoming call from an unknown number and he opened the line. Larry Nichols's cheerful voice came over clear with a simple greeting of relief that Walt had taken the call. "I have someone you need to meet. We will be in Aspen for three days and she would like to meet you both, have lunch and talk a bit the day after tomorrow. Can you meet us at the Hotel Jerome bar at noon and we will find a place where we can talk privately about the Fortuna diamond," Larry saying all this quickly.

Walt looked at Suz as he said they would be there at noon and closed the phone call. "You could hear all that?" Walt asked, then quickly added, "This is a link to some of the missing time our Hazelnut spent from Prince Ibrahim's pocket until it was found on the finger of the mystery woman who wore it as costume jewelry. My guess is this is that woman."

They sat close together on the foot of the bed, Suz afraid to speak her mind and Walt not wanting to tell her what he was thinking. He finally said the obvious, "This is where we will find out why someone wants to control the information about the Fortuna diamond's provenance. There may be a great deal of money, or liability, in having that provenance exposed. Maybe a multi-million dollar decline of value. What I can't answer is why we should even care other than to just satisfy our own curiosity. It could be something entirely different, as if the diamond had been stolen from from someone still living, or that they think we are blackmailers seeking a big payday."

Suz started to laugh as she watched Walt struggling with what seemed to her to be a no win situation which needed to be left alone. Make the meeting, learn what the trip this small piece of ice had taken, leave it be and find some other adventure. "It won't be that easy, will it? To find out and act as if it makes no difference to us. It could make a big difference to the Musson Jewellers. We better be careful where this goes," was Suz's suggestion. Her next suggestion was that it was time to climb into this welcoming bed.

The next morning dawned perfect with a clear blue sky and a brisk fall temperature. They walked to Nick's house and were greeted by him and hustled into the kitchen where Len was putting the first french toast slices in the hot skillet. Five minutes later they were seated with cold, fresh orange juice and just brewed coffee as the first plates were placed. Suz said it first, and Walt agreed, "This is the best french toast I have ever eaten! Len, you do have the touch."

Breakfast was completed with one last cup of coffee taken on the porch and then Nick excused himself as he had some things to attend to in his office nook. Len guided Walt and Suz to his shop which was one of the two large closets in his bedroom. The town homes had originally been designed as luxury guest cottages with two large master bedrooms. The small additional bedroom was used for Nick's office and shared the common bathroom to the house. Everything was top of the line and made for very comfortable permanent residences.

Three stools were in place in front of the work bench and numerous small cabinets lined the wall behind it. The tools of the diamond cutter's trade covered the bench. Len had Walt and Suz take the stools on the outside and he positioned himself on the middle one. His first comment was asking to see Suz's ring. "Don't take it off, just let me have your hand."

He held her hand, obviously enjoying the touch, raised it up to his face and at the same time positioned his loupe over his left eye. A close examination from several angles had him lower the loupe and looking into Suz's eyes telling her, "This is a fine diamond. The best. A Type IIa and the cutting and polishing the very best. Albert cut this one. No one could ever match his skill. You are a very fortunate young woman to have this ring. Never take it off." It was said by Len with such emotion that the three sat side by side in silence for several minutes.

"Now let me show you how this is done. Just the technique, the doing would take weeks, if not more." He demonstrated some faceting on the pavilion, or bottom, of a small diamond he was working on. A machine held the tool mounted diamond at an angle to the abrasive wheel and with light pressure he pressed it gently on the spinning surface. He removed the holder from the machine and carefully checked what he had just done. With a minor adjustment the operation was repeated as the diamond had been rotated a set number of degrees and the cutting repeated. After about three of these steps he removed the holder, cleaned the diamond off with a damp towel and held it under a large magnifying glass so they could see the very small enlargement of the facet to those next to them. "Over and over again and I will have eight equal facets around the pavilion. Many more will be needed to meet the requirements for a brilliant round, the same type as Suz's beautiful stone."

It seemed that Len had lost his place in showing his cutting technique and Walt took this opportunity to take out a top view photo of the Fortuna diamond mounted as a ring. He had made this particular print reversing the image and setting the size to be exactly the size of the diamond. He handed it to Len.

"This is the Fortuna 26.29 carat diamond. You are familiar with the story, aren't you?" was asked in a manner that required no answer and Walt then slipped the ring that Albert had given him two days ago out of it's leather pouch and handed it to Len. "You know what this is, don't you?"

Len sat perfectly still and a look of desperation

came over his face. Suz didn't know what to do, or say, as she had been as surprised by what Walt had just done as was Len. She and Walt had experimented with comparing the ring Albert had given them with the photographs of the Fortuna ring and although the diamonds couldn't be judged to be the same with one hundred percent certainty it was easy to conclude that the rings were. The girdle that hides the pavilian of the big diamond was unique and identical. They hadn't discussed this with anyone yet and she hadn't realized that Walt had put together the comparison photographs.

Len didn't say a word as he positioned the ring's prong tips on the reversed photo's prong positions. It was a perfect match. He finally looked up at Walt and managed to say in a whisper, "That is the Hazelnut diamond. You have found it after all these years. It still exists."

"Albert has the drawing his grandfather made for this ring if Tiffany decided to mount the Hazelnut as a ring instead of in the necklace's pendant. He told us that two had been cast but the other one had disappeared. The ring in the Fortuna photo is it."

Just then Nick came into the room and announced they had less than an hour before their tee time so they should get ready to go over to the Club. Walt put his hand on Len's shoulder and told him that they could have a talk about the ring at dinner. "Interesting, isn't it?" was asked. Len smiled, the color coming back into his face. and he started to quietly laugh as he answered, "Yes it is! Yes, it certainly is!"

# Chapter 40

As Walt pulled into the parking space at the Club an attendant had a cart in place and minutes later he and Suz were at the practice area. Nick was there and was starting his warm up hitting a wedge to a nearby faux green. Walt and Suz followed suit. The air was almost sparkling, the sky a mountain blue and the morning chill just changing to a perfect fall, daytime temperature. Even the golf shots sounded right as they progressed up through the clubs. About five with the drivers and it was time to head for the first tee. They stood together looking at the downhill par five and then at exactly 11:47 am Suz was offered the first tee. They would play even, the Nassau format of first nine, second nine and eighteen at twenty dollars each. No presses. Nick had offered Suz strokes but she declined and he would be glad as it saved him some embarrassment.

The eighteen at Castle Pines is a pleasure to the eye and even better to play. Every hole has some unique twist to keep the golfer's attention on every shot. This day the special hole that they would each remember was number eleven. It is carded at 175 yards but plays 20 yards less as the green is around a seventy feet below the tee. The green is sloped severely downhill from back to front with a creek bordering the left side and front, dammed to from two narrow ponds. At the aim point at the top left of the green is a small sand trap which if your ball ends up there you have a harrowing downhill landing area that begs for mistakes no matter where the pin is placed. Suz, who had just pocketed the first nine money, had the honors from her par on ten. She had chosen two clubs less for the shot but pulled it long and left beyond the trap. Walt was short but escaped going in the water by a few feet. Nick was to the right, just off the green, but not in a bad spot. Suz was away and the pin was positioned in the front of the green, just where it finally leveled out. It was an impossible shot to get close. Even just to stay on the putting surface.

Walt had already learned to never underestimate Suz in anything she chose to do and he stood near his ball and waited, loving every minute he could spend with her. Nick was waiting for a disaster as he had had this shot a number of times and had never been able to save his par. Suz had taken a little extra time, then took her stance and neatly clipped a shot over the trap that landed softly on the spot she had picked. One small bounce and the sixty foot roll began. First across the green then slowly bending to the right picking up speed on the fall line towards the pin. At this point all three knew it was a good shot and the closer it got to the pin the better it was looking. The last turn of the ball saw it disappear into the cup. All three were speechless. Suz had taken two wedges up to her ball and turned to pick the one up she had laid off to the side when she started to smile. Walt and Nick finished the hole with pars down two strokes each on the back nine after only two holes played.

On the tee at twelve Nick asked Suz to marry him and Walt suggested that he and she get married that after- noon. The day ended with drinks at the bar. Suz took the three twenties from each of the two boys and after excusing herself for a few minutes returned from the pro shop wearing a beautiful Castle Pine's green cashmere V-neck sweater. It had the attractive embroidered hummingbird club logo and the gold chain with the small coin showed nicely on her lightly tanned skin. She was holding her golf shirt in one hand and her movements as she approached their table and sat down would be remembered by both Walt and Nick as clearly as how she had played eleven a few hours before.

Len had reserved a table for dinner at the club and they were seated promptly. A number of members stopped by to say hello to Nick but it was obvious they wanted a better look at the lady that had taken his money. Len had been told of the day's events and was enjoying watching his son get a good ribbing. He was also enjoying looking at Suz.

They ordered from of the evening's specials and were very satisfied with their choices. It was decided dessert would be ice cream at home with a cappuccino. It had been a great day and Suz was as happy as Walt had seen her thus far in their relationship. He was more in love with her than ever and for the first time in years felt totally content. Tomorrow was to be a different kind of day.

# Chapter 41

Walt and Suz had packed and after a quick look about the guest cottage they locked the door and drove the short way to Nick's place. Len had fixed a nice breakfast for them of scrambled eggs and toast, sided with fresh strawberries. Orange juice to start and excellent coffee served from a carafe.

As they prepared to leave, Suz gave Len a hug and told him to call Albert as soon as they left. She also said, with laughter in her voice, "Tell him you fell in love with me and you think I am in love with you. He will know what you are saying and maybe it will break some ice that needs to be broken. You are both special people and have too much to share to not be close again."

Len looked in Suz's eyes as his own eyes filled with moisture. "You know, both of you, that Nick is Robert's half brother. It is not what you think. It was my fault not being able to father a child with my beloved Rebecca and we decided that Albert would help us. By we, I mean the four of us. It may have been a rather sophomoric attempt at artificial insemination, but it worked. It also ruined our relationship. Albert left Tiffany to go out on his own and he, Loretta and Robert moved out to Los Angeles just after Nick was born. After only one year it was obvious who Nick's father had been and we had not thought about how this would harm our friendships."

Walt shook hands with Len and softly commented, "Nick and Robert both seem so talented and such good people. I assume they both know their story and they should be closer. You and Albert should see to it that it happens. Loretta is showing signs of dementia and Albert will soon be alone, as are you. Suz and I want to become part of both of your last years and it would be nice if it would work out that way. The Hazelnut diamond is bringing us all together and we need to take advantage of that."

Another hug from Suz and handshake from Walt had Len waving a good-bye from his porch as the Wagoneer went down the drive and then out of sight. He went inside and entered Albert's number on his phone.

Heading out the gate and turning right had them soon on Highway 85 going north with a peek view of two of the front nine holes they had played yesterday. They were leaving a place that had provided them some very good memories and they both hoped they could return for another visit.

Passing by Sedalia had them finding some morning traffic. By the time they joined Interstate 470 heading west they knew they would not make it to the Hotel Jerome bar by twelve noon. Walt handed his phone to Suz and asked to press call back. The phone was on speaker and rang three times but no one answered. Walt said in a clear voice, "see you about one" and indicated that Suz should close the phone.

"You, we, are not back with your group again are we?" was asked by Suz in a accusative manner and she waited for an answer. "No, I am just using a protocol that is used with this group and only to let Larry know we will be late. He will understand exactly what I meant and it won't change any plans. We can still go to Aspen via Independence Pass. Have you ever gone over the Pass?" was asked in a kidding way as he knew if she hadn't it would be a great new experience for her.

Suz was smiling and reached over the console to rub his thigh in a suggestive manner. "Going to show me something new, are you? I think this going to be a good day, after all."

Through the Eisenhower Tunnel and down the long grade. Then through Silverthorne with a nice view of a section of the Blue River. It was then on towards Copper Mountain, where just before getting there they turned south on Highway 91 towards Leadville.

Suz's comment on this being the hometown of the Molly Brown that was unsinkable brought a smile from Walt. He asked if she was familiar with another of Leadville's daughters, Baby Doe Tabor and she acknowledged she had heard the name

"Both were attractive, young and poor. J.J. Brown was a mining engineer that had come to Leadville after a number of other starts in Colorado, including Aspen. He found Margret Tobin there and they were soon married, still poor but in love. By 1893, just before the collapse of the price silver due the demonetization by the government, he had become a board member of the Ibex Mining company and awarded a twelve and a half percent ownership. Following the crash most of the mining for silver was over in Leadville, but there was gold and copper in the Ibex's Little Johnny Mine. Thanks to J. J. the mine was opened up to become one of the biggest in the world. All became rich beyond belief, including J.J. and Molly. It was her trip returning from a European tour aboard the Titanic that earned her the nickname, Unsinkable." By the time Walt had recited this bit of history they had driven through Leadville.

"Then there is Baby Doe. Not a happy story but again a beautiful young woman finding a second marriage to a very rich man twice her age. When the crash came he lost all his wealth and passed away. The fable is that he told Baby Doe to never sell the Matchless Mine and she spent her last thirty years in a small cabin at the mine. After a snow storm in March, 1935 she was found  frozen to death in her bed. She was  eighty-one years old." Walt finished the story saying they should make a visit to Leadville some time and go see the sights, including Baby Doe Tabor's little cabin. Suz responding with a simple, "I think not!"

Highway 91 turns into 24 and in a few miles the eastern terminus of the famous Highway 82 is taken heading west to Aspen. The climb to the Pass is one of the great mountain drives and the view from there demands a stop and short walk to take it all in. It was Suz's first visit and she held Walt's hand tight as she said, "You take me to the nicest places. Don't ever stop doing this!"

# Chapter 42

The trip down was as exciting as the trip up had been. Vistas and many views of the Roaring Fork River as it becomes a river. Entering Aspen brought reality back and soon they were on the streets of a bustling resort town. Walt didn't hesitate as he passed the Hotel Jerome on Main Street, turned left on South Aspen Street and parked next to Paepcke Park. Two other cars were parallel parked there and he pulled in the space left behind them. They had ten minutes to walk back to the Jerome Bar.

Suz made no comment on why he went this far past the hotel, even though it was just a short walk back. They used the restrooms first and then walked into the bar together at exactly one o'clock. Larry was seated with an attractive woman, who looked to be in her sixties, at one of the tables in the back corner of the room farthest from the Main Street windows. He stood, welcomed them both and introduced Sally Mayfield. She shook Suz's hand first and then gave Walt a bit too long handshake making an obvious appraisal of who it was she was meeting.

They took their seats, the draft beers were ordered, quickly served and the lunch choices made. The drive over was discussed and the conversation was shared equally. Walt suggested that Larry could invite his partner at the end of the bar to join them and he laughed and muttered that he knew Walt would pick up on this but just the four of them were required for this meeting. Lunch was eaton and enjoyed and then Larry said he had a private room secured for the business meeting.

It was a small room just off the hotel lobby, had no windows, a small table and four chairs. It could be a room for a bridge game, high stakes poker or very private conversations. Sally spoke saying only, "Nazli Sabri. Is that name familiar to you?"

Walt and Suz both nodded their heads in the affirmative and she continued, "I was a friend of Princess Fathia's only daughter, Rania Ghali, in Los Angeles. A young friend, both of us still teenagers at the time. I will tell you what I knew about her and her mother before we get to the diamond, which is what I understand you are interested in."

Sally paused and seemed to be lost in thought for a few moments, then continued, "You do understand how the typical Arab man treated women in the past. Especially those men in powerful positions. Even commoner relationships still have this treatment of women today. At the time of Nazli's marriage to King Fuad she was isolated from the royal life until after she bore him a son, Farouk. She then bore four daughters, about one every two years, the youngest Fathia. Nazli was well educated and having strong ideas of how women should be treated rebelled against the treatment of women, much to her determent. After Fuad's death in 1936 she found love with Ahmed Hassanein Pasha, one of the new King's, her son Farouk, advisors. She wasn't allowed to marry him as it was thought to be disrespectful to the royal family. He was later killed in an automobile accident and Nazli was left to be a very unhappy Queen Mother. She had one thing to fall back on in that she was never kept from buying and keeping jewelry and she never had any qualms in doing so. She was once thought to have the largest and most valuable collection of jewelry in the world."

Again Sally took a pause, then continued. "In 1946 Nazli came to America to have treatment for a serious kidney ailment and never returned to Egypt. Fathia came with her, as did the third daughter, Faika. The oldest daughter, Fawzia, married the man who became the King of Iran.

"Nazli had brought with her a fine wardrobe and of course her jewelry collection. It including the Hazelnut pendant." As she said this last she could see that Walt and Suz, even knowing much of which she had been telling them, were now in full attention.

"Nazli did not waste much time in Los Angeles before living her life in an extravagant way. Faika was first to marry, by her own choice to a commoner Egyptian, in 1950 and it was reluctantly acceptable to her brother, King Farouk. Fathia's marriage to Riyad Ghali Effendi was not acceptable to him and he then deprived the Queen Mother and her daughter of all their rights and titles. This also included their income and property in Egypt. It was here that Nazli's financial difficulties began as she used her jewelry as collateral to by a 28-room mansion in Beverly Hills where she lived with Fathia, her husband and their three children. By the early 1970s they had squandered most of their wealth, were in bankruptcy and living in small apartments. Fathia had divorced Riyad, and the children were young adults. All of them lived nearby and Fathia was again living with her mother. It was here Nazli's life fell apart. In 1976 the President of Egypt, Anwar Sadat, gave them passports to return to Egypt and the plans were made to do this. The day they were to return, December 10th, 1976, Fathia had gone to her ex-mother-in-law's apartment to get something she wished to take with her and found Riyad, who was living there, drunk. They had an argument and he killed her with multiple shots from a revolver and then, unsuccessfully, tried to kill himself. There was a one column article in the December 13, 1976 New York Times describing the event, with a photo of Fathia, and titled Sister of Farouk Is Killed; Husband Is Held."

Sally's face took on a totally different look as she prepared to give them the answers they were waiting for. She cleared her throat and started her story, "When the auction of the remaining jewelry of both Nazli and Fathia failed to realize enough to settle the bankruptcy court that September their plans to return to Egypt were made. That morning, the day Fathia had been murdered, Nazli called me to come to her apartment immediately. I did and she invited me in, told me nothing about what she had just learned of Fathia's death and gave me a small leather pouch. She told me this was the last jewel she had left and had hidden it from the bankruptcy court. I was to take it and never tell anyone who gave it to me. She told me that somctime earlier she had contacted a young diamond cutter in Beverly Hills to take the Hazelnut pendant and mount the big diamond into a ring and see if he could distribute some of the value of the smaller diamonds to Fathia's children. I was to keep the ring hidden until I thought it to be safe to wear it in public. It had to be hidden for a while as it would be quickly recognized as the Hazelnut diamond. The diamond cutter had given her his word that he would never reveal how he came into possession of the pendant."

She paused for a moment, then said in a whisper, "I know he has kept his word. Not many would have."

The four of them in the small windowless room, just off the lobby of he Hotel Jerome, sat silently with Walt and Suz having just received the answers to their questions. As to the future of this diamond as Fortuna, they had no interest. Still, it wasn't quite over for them as something still did not seem quite right in the provenience of the Hazelnut and it wouldn't be long before they would be searching for answers again.

Nazli died on May 26, 1978 at the age of 83 in Los Angeles after a long and painful illness.

# Chapter 43

Walt and Suz said their thank yous and goodbyes to Larry and Sally in the lobby. Sally was staying the rest of the week in Aspen, at the St. Regis Hotel, and Larry was flying back to Washington D.C. that afternoon.

They walked around town for about an hour trying to decide whether to spend the night in Aspen or drive part way back to Dubois. It was 475 miles and it was almost three o'clock. Neither felt like being a tourist and Aspen no longer seemed to have the appeal they remembered from the earlier visits they had made to ski.

It was back at the Wagoneer that things began to come into focus, especially for Suz. Walt had asked her to go over to the Gazebo for a minute as he walked around the car. The telltales were intact on the doors and the rear window hatch. He had been able to put the ones on the two front doors without Suz noticing after they had parked the car. The others he had placed before they left Castle Pines. They were about the same color as the paint and didn't show unless you knew what to look for. The one on the hood was missing.

He walked over to the Gazebo, up onto the platform where Suz was waiting, and he knew she knew what was going on. He was pleased at that but sorry with what was about to happen.

"Tell me what is going on! I mean tell me right

now, Wainwright!" was said in a way that he had to tell her, so he did. "The telltale on the hood is missing. Someone opened it while we were in the hotel. I can't be sure because the driver's door one is still in place and once you remove the telltale you can't use it again. It won't stick. I have to open the hood and take a look. I want you to stay here until I wave you to come over to the car." Walt said this in a voice Suz was not used to hearing and just merely nodded her head in an okay. Her face told Walt exactly what he was fearing.

He didn't hesitate opening the driver's side door and popping the hood latch. It partially opened and he waited one minute. If it was to happen it would have done so immediately. Raising the hood didn't result in any kind of detonation and Walt looked in on the driver's side of the engine. He saw nothing on the number one spark plug wire, likewise none on three. It was there on number five and just a small clip with a single wire leading to the master brake cylinder. A small wrap of plastic explosive which would puncture, or at least damage the seal of the brake fluid line to all four brakes. Walt removed the plastic easily and the clip from the ignition wire putting them into his pocket. He inspected the passenger side wires and then closed the hood.

He went back to Suz and told her in an unemotional tone, "It isn't over. At worst, that would cause an inconvenience unless emergency braking was necessary. The emergency brake is not affected and you could drive on for miles using it until you find a mechanic to do the repair. I have no idea the why, or whether it was Larry or Sally that may have had it installed. Larry's friend at the bar had plenty of time to install it and I saw he had a full glass of beer in front of him when we came out of our meeting. How either of them could know where we had parked is another question needing an answer. Let's get out of here and we will stop for the night when it is time."

Suz said nothing and when Walt turned the key the engine started and sounded right. It was a warning and not meant to be a kill.  Walt was used to this and turned to Suz taking her left hand in his. "I expect to be holding this hand with the diamond ring on the ring finger for years to come. Don't make more of this than a warning that we should go no further with Hazel," was said in a reassuring way. Suz answered, "Until death do us part, okay," and her tears started to fall.

For the next thirty minutes no words were spoken until they reached Basalt and the sign denoting the Frying Pan river was spotted by Suz. She asked Walt to take the road that went up towards Rudi Reservoir along it. "This is supposed to be a gold medal trout stream. Lets see if we see anything we might want to come back here to visit." It was asked in a now clear voice, free of any fear or doubt.

# Chapter 44

Walt did as asked and ten minutes later he pulled over to a parking spot on the river's side. There were five identically outfitted students being given instructions by a handsome and tanned young man. It was obvious all them were getting their first lessons as the casting was not going well. Driving a few miles farther found every parking pull off filled with cars and pickups and the river crowded with fishermen. "No thank you, mister Wainwright. A little space by Ollie's place on the Wind River will do me just fine."

Two hours later they had pulled into the parking area of the Blue Spruce Inn in Meeker, Colorado and in ten minutes had a room for the night. Carl's Burgers, four blocks away, was chosen for dinner and soon they were sitting at a small table for two with hamburgers and fries platted and tall milk shakes on the side. Strawberry for Suz and chocolate for Walt. It was a good choice for dinner.

Back in the motel room Suz had sat on the edge of the bed and was looking at Walt in a way he was becoming accustomed. She wanted some answers. He sat down next to her and had instinctively pulled the wired plastic assembly out of his pocket. He took a second, more careful look at what he had stuffed into his pocket in Aspen. The clip was attached over the insulation of the wire, not on the bare wire. It couldn't have detonated. The detonator was a real one but when he examined the plastic, it was just clay that looked like the explosive but was just a decoy.

Holding the set up for Suz to look at he said, "This is just a decoy. The plastic is just a clay look alike and the clip is wired so there is no way it could set off the detonater. It is a fake and harmless. It was used only to send a message to stop any further search for Hazel."

"You make my life so exciting. First you may be killed, taking me along with you, just to make us stop looking for a special little diamond given to a silent movie star by a second rate Egyptian prince over a hundred years ago. Can life get any better than that!" Suz's laughter was contagious and Walt reached for her as they tumbled backward onto the bed.

It was decided that it would be better to wait until tomorrow morning but once in the shower together that decision was changed. Sleep then came easily and they slept in until seven. It was Saturday, October 7th and the world was about to change as the coverage from Israel was on the morning news. Suz, who Walt had never heard swear before said, "Those God damn Arabs!"

It was eight hours to Dubois and they pulled in just before dark. The van was now home and they were glad to get there. The news in the Middle East was getting worse by the hour. It seemed that peace there, and in most of north Africa, was only allowed to last fifteen to twenty years before one conflict or another would spring up. The Sudan was in tatters with violence and poverty, Iran appeared to be financing much of this mayhem through out the area, apparently including Hamas in Gaza and Hezbollah in Lebanon. Even factions in Turkey were promoting revolt. Turkey, which just two decades ago was considered one of the must visit countries for tourists, was verging on armed conflict and no longer recommended to U.S. citizens for travel. Even Egypt was exhibiting unrest again. Suz started singing the words of the old Kingston Trio song once more, "The whole world is festering with unhappy souls, the French hate the Germans; the Germans hate the Poles, and I don't like anybody very much."

The tears came next. "How can humans treat each other this way. The Palestinians have something to be offended by with the settlement of the Jewish state but not enough to warrant what they just did.  What is wrong with these people?" was asked as if she was alone.

Walt offered that it had to do with cultures, how they ascended with enormous progress, then fell with almost unbelievable speed. Following the ups and down of Egypt during their search for Hazel had shown these trends and he thought America was now beginning a decent which was accelerating under the current administration and said in a discouraged manner,  "Our open borders will lead us to economic ruin, especially for all the big cities as they are forced to support the new emigrants who have no way to support themselves. The children will need education and most speak no English. The already over burdened health care system will become over whelmed and end up collapsing. This will only end in one way, very, very badly."

Suz then surprised Walt when she asked, "Could we buy your old cabin?" Walt did not have to ask why as he was thinking along the same lines.

# Chapter 45

Sunday morning dawned with a beautiful fall sunrise in Dubois, Wyoming but the news from the Middle East cast a pall that seemed to blot out all that was good in the world. Adding to this was the sense that in their own life what should have been the finish of a relatively unimportant search for the story of the Hazelnut diamond had not yet been concluded in a satisfactory way.

Suz said the obvious as they lay together in bed after wakening that morning. "Sally's story was too perfect, almost rehearsed. Did you get that impression?" she asked with the assurance that Walt would agree with her.

He rolled over toward her and smiled at having someone that thought out complex things as he did. Just as he started to speak his phone chirped his incoming call melody. He reached for the phone, didn't recognize the number but answered anyway with a simple "Yes!"

"Walt, it's Larry. I am on a secure line and need to give you a heads up. After our meeting I wanted to ask Sally Mayfield a few more questions and went over to the Saint Regis. She was not registered as a guest and a call to the airport disclosed she had flown out an hour earlier with a connecting flight to LAX. She had flown in that morning. No three day vacation in Aspen with time to meet and tell me her story. You and Suz's inclusion was, in retrospect, now understandable. She had known of your involvement in the search and this should have tipped me off that some thing more than my search was why she had contacted me."

A pause let Walt ask about his buddy at the bar and there was an even longer pause. Then, "He wasn't with me. I am pretty sure he was with Sally. Doesn't add up either. What are you thinking?"

It was Walt's turn to pause and he could see the fear cross Suz's face. "Larry, I don't think we are finished with this project. He left me a present on the Wagoneer's master brake cylinder. Only a decoy, but the message was clear. I first thought it was your way of telling us to back off. I am glad it wasn't and I think we have another path to take. Maybe join up on this. It is the years leading up to the day Fathia Ghali, Nazli's youngest daughter, was murdered and then on to the present."

Larry quickly voiced agreement with the opinion and offered that they should meet in person to compare some notes. "Maybe it is time for me to make another visit to Dubois. Dinner up at the cabin," was suggested by Larry with enough double meaning in his voice to bring a smile to Walt's face while Suz's showed the recognition with what was being said between the two men.

Walt had the phone on speaker so she had heard the entire conversation. After the connection was broken Suz sat up, turning to Walt, and smiled. "Don't just lay there, we have plans to make, but first tell me what you are thinking. Fathia didn't go to her ex-mother-in-laws apartment, where her ex-husband was living, to get some of her mother-in-laws clothes the day she and Nazli were flying back to Egypt. Their suitcases and trunks were already packed. She wanted something small and valuable that she was sure was hidden there."

Walt wouldn't argue with that so he suggested  that they get dressed, fix a breakfast to take down to their table on the river and go over what they now both suspected. With bowls of cereal prepared and a thermos of coffee they were soon sitting at their special spot enjoying the river as it flowed past unconcerned with anything in the human world. In that special way it helped quiet their own concerns.

After they had finished with breakfast, and fixed their second cups of coffee, Walt started his summarizing of what he was now thinking. There was now an even bigger piece of missing jewelry that he thought had just come into play and it was this that was causing the warnings to them to leave their search.

"I think we have to examine the lowest points in Nazli's life. First the Sotheby auction of her jewelry including her favorite pieces of jewelry, the Van Cleef and Arpels tiara and necklace, in November, 1975. This sale was not enough to cover her debts and a second auction of her and Fathia's remaining jewelry was scheduled by the bankruptcy court in September, 1976. Then came the murder of Fathia by her ex-husband on December 10, 1976, the day she and Fathia were supposed to have returned to Egypt. Nazli was already in declining health by this time and she died in pain, alone and with a broken heart less than two years later."

Walt paused and Suz nodded for him to continue as she agreed and was sure she knew what was coming next. "The sale of their remaining jewelry in 1976 and the disappearance of the Van Cleef and Arpels tiara are the keys. The necklace resurfaced in a 2015 Sotheby,s auction but the tiara has never been found. That is our key in solving this mystery and I think we both can guess where it is now?" Walt had asked this last for Suz to answer.

"Albert Morgan!" was her answer. She then added, "The necklace was sold for $140,000 and the tiara for $127,500 at the 1975 auction. In the 2015 auction the necklace sold for $4,282,000. Van Cleef and Arpels was the buyer to use it in exhibitions and as an investment. What they would pay for the matching tiara can only be guessed, but the two together would be worth much more than separated."

Walt could not suppress his smile. Suz had realized exactly what he had just described and also knew how much danger Albert could now be in. He had taken the Hazelnut pendant from Nazli and built her the ring to carry as a low value piece of jewelry sometime earlier. She had given it to Sally Mayfield the morning when Fathia hadn't come back and she feared that something had gone wrong. Fathia hadn't gone to Riyad Ghail mother's apartment to collect some of her clothes. She had been murdered by Riyad by the time Nazli got there and she had to have stepped over her beloved daughter's body to search for the tiara. Riyad was also there, having shot himself in attempted suicide, but he had even failed in doing that and was laying on the floor unconscious. She must have found the tiara and taken it directly to Albert. There was no way she could take it with her to Egypt, as it would have been discovered and confiscated. Still in bankruptcy court she couldn't keep it in her own apartment.

Young Rayed Ghali. the middle child of Fathia and Riyad, would find the bodies of his parents that afternoon.

# Chapter 46

Walt, looking at Suz, dialed in Albert's number and his call was answered on the second ring. "Hi Walt, I trust it is you," surprised him but he told him that he and Suz would like to drive over for a visit and they would be leaving that afternoon and drive straight through. Would that be okay?

Albert didn't hesitate, and there was a hint of fear in his voice, "I think that is a good idea. Nothing has happened on this end but there seems to be a little too much auto traffic on our street the last two days. Maybe I am paranoid, but I can sense something bad is about to happen. I am guessing that you and Suz have discovered what happened here the day my friend Nazli's daughter was killed by her ex-husband. I may be in a little spot of trouble and you may not have time for any golf. I need some help. I didn't want it to end up this way," Albert said and broke the connection.

The look on Suz's face had them both head up to the van, pack a suitcase and this time when she saw Walt place his gun and three clips in his ever present duffel bag she showed no disapproval. They stopped at their bank and using a personal check got two thousand in cash. It would take at least another day to have the record in their account show up. The Wagoneer had a full tank of gas and by 12:30 they were on the road. Gas and meals were paid for in cash. Jack and Ollie were asked that if anyone inquired about their whereabouts that they had just gone off to camp out for a few days.

At four o'clock the next day they turned into Albert's driveway. He had opened the garage door and waved them into the vacant space. The garage door was closed behind them and they exited to a warm greeting from Albert. He directed them directly into his office and shop area and had them seated on the same stools as before. Albert then went to his safe and came back into the dimly lit space setting the Van Cleef and Arpels tiara, glistening under the spot light, in front of them.

"It is exactly as it was the day Nazli brought it to me, the afternoon of December 10, 1976. Every one of the 720 diamonds, 274 carats in total, are there. She never mentioned what had just happened and told me to keep it as long as I could. That her planned return to Egypt with Fathia that evening had to be canceled and she wasn't sure what was to become of her. The next day everyone, at least here in California, knew what had happened. I helped support her financially until her death, and helped clear some of her and Fathia's debts, anonymously, afterwards. Another donor had done much more than I but we took care of what was needed. I have no idea of who it was but I suspect it was he who bought the tiara at the Sotheby auction in 1975 and gave it back to her."

Nothing more could be said as the beauty of the tiara couldn't be ignored. Eventually Suz broke the spell, commenting, "Men, or women, would do almost anything to possess such beauty as this and they have done so and will continue to do so. Albert, we three are all in danger at this moment. Walt will explain this and we have some plans on what we should do."

"Let me get you settled. In your old room which is now yours until Loretta and I are gone. I need this," motioning with one hand at the tiara, "out of our lives. I did not know what to do with it then and I don't know what to do with it now."

It was at dinner, the same supplied by the Italian delicatessen on their last visit, that Loretta seemed aware of their guests and joined in the conversation occasionally. Her offhand comment that would be remembered was when she commented on how Albert had treated their Egyptian royalty. It had been more than just the visit the day of Fathia's death. Nazli had visited a number of times before and afterwards. Albert had been with her the day she had died in the hospital. "Nazli was too old to be his mother and he was too young to be her lover. It was a good relationship for him at the time and it didn't bother me in the least," was said by Loretta as if it had happened just last week instead of over forty-five years ago.

All four retired by nine and Walt and Suz were in bed by nine-thirty, comfortable but wide awake. Walt started the conversation reciting some of the happenings to the Egypt royalty during World War II and of the coup of 1952 exiling the dynasty of Mohammad Ali from Egypt. During World War II Egypt had become a major Allied base for the North African campaign and other decisions by the young King Farouk, including not challenging the British desires to continue their control of the Suez canal, caused the Egyptian nationalists to start thinking about his removal. Losses of a large portion of Palestine in the unsuccessful Palestine war of 1948-1949 exacerbated the discontent. The Free Officer Movement had formed around a young leader, Gamal Abdel Nasser and joining them was a war hero, General Mohammed Naguib, which attracted even more militant followers. By 1953 the royal family had left Egypt with just what they could take with them. They were able to take enough for all to live out their lives in luxury.

In a more conversational manor he told Suz, "Our young Prince Ibrahim, by then was fifty-three and properly married to a granddaughter of Padishah Abdelhamid, the last of Ottoman Sultans. His brother, Amr, had married one of her sisters. Before the war the two brothers bought properties in a rural area, Maadi, southwest of Cairo on the eastern bank of the Nile. The war had them in Switzerland for it's duration and Ibrahim, during this time, designed his Moresque mansion. Upon his return after the war he built his dream villa surrounded by a beautiful two acre garden. Both the brothers villas were confiscated by the state in 1954 and their contents looted. After years of misuse Ibrahim's villa was abandoned and was described as turned into a dump heap and home only to bats, rodents, stray cats and rabid dogs. The area later became Garden City, a very poor suburb of Cairo."

Suz rolled over to lay against Walt, needing his arms around her. "How sad, but they did it to themselves. In power they took advantage of all those under their control. Looting and mismanaging their country to their own benefit until a rebellion took control with no experience in how to build or run a country. Is this what is happening, here in our country?" was asked of Walt in a sad voice.

"Yes," was Walt's one word answer and he reached for his phone. He punched in a number and on the first ring Larry answered asking,"What and where?" Walt replied, "I need two body guards, 24 hours a day for at least three days. The best." Larry asked, "Do I know where?" and Walt replied, "Yes. Nine tomorrow morning," and the connection was broken.

Suz didn't move, just holding Walt even tighter and whispering in his ear, "You, we, are back into it. How can this be happening? Who is the enemy this time?" She was not frightened and Walt at that moment knew he had to make good on this rescue because it was the only way out of what they had gotten themselves into. Just an old piece of jewelry once made famous by those of the past who had no right to have possessed it in the first place. It was now worth six million dollars, or maybe even more.

# Chapter 47

At nine o'clock sharp a four year old panel van with faded Jake Smith House Painting signage on both sides, including a telephone number, drove up and stopped in front of Albert Morgan's house. On top two well used ladders were strapped on the carrier. Both doors opened and the two men exited the van, one older, both in white coveralls that were clean but showing considerable wear. The older man went to the door as the younger retrieved the smaller of the ladders from the carrier.

Albert greeted the older man at the front door and they went inside but were quickly back as the younger had started placing painting equipment on the porch. In less than ten minutes all were inside and the front door was closed behind them. Introductions were made and now Walt and Suz were standing with the group. Walt and the older man knew each other and their greeting was of an old friendship based on much different circumstances than house painting. Walt knew who he was dealing with and said a silent thank you to Larry.

Two street side bedrooms were staged to be painted and within thirty minutes drop clothes were being placed, buckets, paint pails, a small table set up and two special tool boxes lay on the floor to one side. The curtains were drawn to the side and then taken down. The window framing was taped with blue tape and the glass then covered with a paper that was clear from the inside but opaque as viewed from the outside.

Loretta was introduced and the conversation was not on the house painting but how the guarding would be set up. By days end, with a second Jake Smith van arriving mid-day for a quick stop, Albert's house had two very fit young men in place that were dressed in white coveralls having a different cut that obscured a fully loaded military type belts. When the remaining Jake Smith van left the house at five o'clock that afternoon it would seem to most observers that the painting crew had left. That was not the case and Gary and Hal had the bedroom downstairs next to Albert's office and workshop. They made themselves familiar with the access points, the stairs to the main floor from either end of the house, the elevator and with the entire property.

Walt was more than satisfied. He knew what was required here in the house and these men knew what needed to be done to be ready for any possible intrusion. They had all the supplies they would require, including food, and would raise no suspicions of them being embedded.

At two o'clock that afternoon Walt and Suz prepared to make a visit to the Sotheby showroom, located nearby on North Camden Drive. They placed two cloth grocery bags in the back of the Wagoneer that were stuffed with rolled up paper but looked from a distance to be filled with groceries. If observed returning, carrying the bags would present a trip to the grocery store. As they pulled out of the garage, closing the door with the door fob Albert had given them, they headed toward downtown Beverly Hills.

"You see the car at the corner, turn toward me and

tell me what a nice day it is. Don't look at the car!" was Walt's command. "I see them, but it is a very nice day," Suz said as she had already turned his way and was patting him on his thigh. She didn't miss Walt's smile as he acknowledged that she knew exactly what to do. It would be tested a few more times over the next week, but he knew he had a partner in tune with what was going on.

They entered the gallery as just tourists with time to kill but as they looked at several of the paintings more carefully Suz explained a bit loudly, "That's by Amina El Demirdash! She is Queen Nazli's great-granddaughter, Princess Faika's granddaughter. How about that, Walt!"

The next moment one of the gallery staff was at their side and was telling them how they had a dozen of her works in a private gallery and would they like to see them. Suz carried the conversation and her explanation of how she was researching royal jewelry collections and those who had amassed and owned them. That Queen Nazli of Egypt had become her favorite study and that she had just found the 2017 Vogue-Arabia article covering Amina wearing the famous Van Cleef and Arpels necklace.

They were quickly escorted into the private show room and a dozen more of the vivid and gloriously colored abstract paintings, each hiding something of a human feature or other surprise. Just an eye, lips, an entire figure that only shows themselves when you step back from the colors. And then there was Mme. Marguerite, 128 – 95 cm dated 2019. "That can't be Queen Nazli?" Suz almost shouted. "Clearly not, but that's what I see. Nazli was a beautiful woman, intelligent, far greater than the King and Princes that were around her. But I guess she was a bit of a shrew."

A very well dressed older gentleman had entered the room and walking up to Suz, smiled and as almost an announcement softly said, "It is so nice to hear you talk of the Egyptian Queen. You know her story, I am sure. You know of her jewelry I think and I would like to talk to you both in private."  Before Suz could answer, he continued, "That is definitely not Queen Nazli my dear, but is as the painting is titled, Mme. Marguerite. You must research her story as she murdered her husband on July 10, 1923 in London, while visiting there from their home in Egypt."

Minutes later they were seated in a very nice office. A right sized desk and several comfortable, over stuffed chairs. Offers of coffee were accepted and then Randolph introduced himself, leaning forward and asked Suz if she recognized the necklace Amina was wearing in the article's photographs.

Walt knew he was not part of this conversation sat back, sipped his coffee and watched Suz play the game.

"That was quite a family. The Queen  commissioning Van Cleef and Arpels to build a necklace and tiara for her to wear at her oldest daughter's, Fawiza, wedding to the man who would become the King of Iran. All fairy tales don't come  out well, as this one didn't, but it was interesting. Also, what ever became of the tiara?"

Randolph sat perfectly still. His face had lost much of it's color and he was intently staring at Suz. "Do you know something I don't?" he whispered. The room was quiet, Suz looked Randolph in the eyes, neither one blinked. He then reached for his phone and punched a speed-dial number. He put the phone on speaker, the voice on the other end only said, "Yes!"

# Chapter 48

The three in the room sat in silence with the echo of "Yes!" in their heads. The voice on the phone finally broke the spell and introduced himself as Theodore Becker, then added with a sense of humor, "That is not my real name. I am a go between for businesses that work together but must keep separated in their dealings. Let me just tell you I co-ordinate between Sotheby and Van Cleef and Arpels. Find something Sotheby can auction that Van Cleef and Arpels wishes to buy or items Van Cleef and Arpels wish to sell at an auction using Sotheby. I am sure you know of Van Cleef and Arpels having the Queen Nazli necklace and that they would certainly like the tiara if it was ever found. I also assume you know how much they had to paid at the auction for the necklace."

Although Theodore could not see his audience he assumed they understood what he was getting at. "There is another that wants in on finding the tiara, if it exists, not because of it's beauty but to be politically annoying. I am speaking of a small group that have found a home in Qatar and whom you do not want to be involved with. They have found a little trouble with their constituents in Gaza at the moment but you cannot trust they won't make a try for the tiara. Again, if it exists."

There was a long pause and Randolph coughed loudly, cleared his throat and asked of Walt and Suz,

"Have you seen it? Do you know where it is? Does it really exist?"

Walt waited and Suz smiled. Finally she said, "Yes, yes, and yes."

Walt then entered the conversation. "We have the tiara. It has been in possession of our client since December 10, 1976. It is untouched from that day and is in the exact condition it was then. Every diamond is the original, in the exact position it was when he received it. He, and we, need protection, and I mean immediately."

Randolph was looking worse and it was Theodore that stepped into the conversation. First he asked Randolph if he would like him to set things up with Sotheby New York and call him back. Randolph first nodded several times in agreement and finally was able to cough out an audible, "Please do."

"Give me one hour. I will call you back. No later than one hour from now," and the connection was broken.

Again there was an awkward silence but the color was coming back into Randolph's face and finally he said in a strained voice, "Theodore knows how to get things done. We can wait here if it is okay with you both."

The hour went by and ten minute late, Theodore was back on the line. "Sotheby New York is flying out two of their top diamond experts and will be in Beverly Hills at ten o'clock tonight. Is the tiara there?" Walt answered in the affirmative and said for them to call the number he gave for his phone when they arrived in front of the Sotheby gallery. They would be ten minutes away and he would give them the address then. Walt also asked that they bring at least two body guards with them.

At 10:30 that evening the call came, the address

given and at 10:45 four men approached Albert Morgan's front door. Two dressed in business suits, ties and jackets, and two nicely dressed but with the all too recognizable look of body guards. Within ten minutes seven people were stationed around the mannequin under the spot light in Albert's dimly lit workroom. Albert returned from his safe, positioned the tiara and there was an audible gasp from the two men dressed in suits as they pressed in closer until they were less than a foot from the sparkling jewelry. They quickly would determine it was indeed the lost Queen Nazli tiara.

With the lights turned up the diamond specialists started their examination. They had several cards with data covering lines and columns. They started a count of certain arrangements of the diamonds and completing each they would say out loud to the room, "Yes." Then the magnifying glasses came and more yeses and more announces of affirmation were verbalized. Last were the loupes and each, in turn, handling the tiara with gloved hands. They passed it back and forth and finally placing it back on the mannequin with care made the final call, "This is the Queen Nazli tiara by Van Cleef and Arpels. One hundred percent certainty!"

Things continued quickly as one of the examiners set his brief case on the table, open it and withdrew a folder. He motioned to Albert to come closer and the offer to handle the auction by Sotheby was laid out. A check, an agreement page and several documents with the fine print of the legalize. "This is all standard agreements for all fine jewelry auctions. The check is for a minimum guarantee and purchase. There are no hidden tricks here. If you would like us to handle the auction and take the tiara with us now only your signature in two places is needed. We have 280 years of unblemished history and I promise everything will be done to satisfy you with our services." The contract was placed in front of Albert and he gazed at it, looking confused, for only a moment. He turned to Suz and asked her to come with him and they headed to his office with the folder.

Albert took a seat in his office chair and Suz stood next him as they spread out the folder's contents on his desk. "I am an old man and this stuff is hard for me to even read, much less understand. I want that tiara gone from my life and I require nothing for it other than it be handled fairly. Will you make the decision for me?" was asked by Albert in a pleading manor.

Suz looked at the check that was made out with no designation. A blank check for one million dollars. The auction agreement read reasonable to Suz and she leafed through the fine print pages without seeing anything that stood out as untoward. "Albert, if I were you I would fill out that check with your company name, sign the papers and say your goodbyes to the tiara. You can figure out what to do with the monies, which will probably be much more than what is on this check, when the auction is completed. Get it done now."

Albert searched around in his desk drawer and pulled out an old stamp and an equally old ink pad. Opening the lid of the ink pad he stamped it several times and then once on a blank sheet of paper. Two more tries finally showed  Gemologist Services of Beverly Hills clearly and he then stamped the line on the check, not even looking at the amount. He signed the two signature lines and asked Suz to take it out to the men waiting in his shop.

Albert made one more trip to his safe and took out a very old box from the shelf. On the top was embossed Van Cleef and Arpels in raised gold script and he slowly went out to where the entire cast of this evenings event were waiting.

Thirty minutes later the Brinks armored truck was being loaded with a special box escorted by all present, even including Loretta tightly holding Albert's hand. The thick steel doors of the truck were closed and the Queen Nazli tiara was on it's way to it's new residence.

The two Sotheby diamond experts made their departure with their bodyguards and at Walt's request Gary and Hal would stay on for two more days. It was ten minutes to one in the morning, October 10, 2023.

Before 2024 could get underway the Queen Nazli necklace and tiara were both in their original presentation box in the vault at Van Cleef and Arpels in Paris, France.

# Chapter 49

Walt and Suz walked with Albert and Loretta to the elevator and rode up to the main floor saying their good nights in the hallway that led to their bedrooms. Walt opened the front door and he and Suz went out onto the front porch. The car at the corner was no longer there and the street was empty and peaceful.

Suz had not let go of Walt's hand since they entered the elevator with Albert and Loretta. As they went back inside and the front door had been closed and locked she turned to him asking, "It is over? Really over now that the tiara is making it way back into the light of day in other hands?"

Walt didn't answer and was forming what he wanted to say as they made their way to their room. Inside he brought her to him, holding her gently and kissing her on her cheek. "We can't be sure. No reason as the tiara is out of Albert's home and will soon be in an other's high security building. It is no longer available from us. Any of us! But our involvement caused the loss to the others that were hoping to profit from it if they had gained it's possession. Some of these are not good people and sometimes revenge is almost as satisfying to them as the possession itself. We can only hope that won't be the case."

Suz stood still enjoying the moment although not with Walt's answer. They readied for bed and as Suz came out of the bathroom, dressed in her light cotton pajamas, the look of love for her that came to Walt's face she now understood and valued more than anything else in her life.

They lay together but sleep would not come for either. Suz turned the small bedside light back on, cuddled up to Walt and whispered in his ear, "You might like to know a little more about our latest acquaintance, Mme Marguerite. Maybe not too much as I don't want you to start dreaming about another woman. Amina El Demirdash's painting is not really a likeness but maybe in those eyes does show her true character."

Suz then ran her hand over Walt's chest and asked in a sexy voice, "Would you like to know more?" She could feel his answer and quickly said, "She murdered her second husband in the Savoy Hotel in London on July 10, 1923 by shooting him multiple times in the back and head after just seven months of marriage."

Suz's teasing had Walt waiting her return and had him thinking of all that had happened in the last two months. His rescue mission had failed, him only able to bring the lifeless body of the victim back and not the vibrant young man that he had tried to rescue. In a gunfight he had killed the three kidnappers and had been himself shot and could have lost his life far away in a gray sea off the shore from a foreign country. It had left him lonely, depressed and thinking there was no real meaning left for him to go on as he was living. Not even five weeks ago he had rescued the proverbial damsel in distress and was now in love with her. He was feeling a wanting to be alive in a way he had  never experienced before.

The next minute she was again laying next to him and saying, "Listen here, you behave yourself now so you can learn the lessons from our Mme Marguerite."

Suz read the opening story from Wikipedia on her iPad, "Marguerite Marie Alibert was born on December 9, 1890, was a French socialite. She started her career as a prostitute and later a courtesan in Paris and from 1917 to 1918, had an affair with the prince of Wales (later Edward VIII). After her marriage to Egyptian aristocrat Ali Kamel Fahmy Bey, she was frequently called princess by the media of the time. In 1923, she killed her husband at the Savoy Hotel in London. She was eventually acquitted of the murder charge after a trial at the Old Bailey."

Suz started laughing and was poking Walt in the ribs adding, "There is more of course. Want me to tell you all the details of this remarkable lady that has now come into our lives?"

"I think you had better if you are suggesting I have something to learn in how to properly treat a lady," Walt answered as he reached for her and pulled her closer.

"Well, our Mme Marguerite was born to a coach-man father and a cleaning lady mother who fortunately worked for the very well to do of Paris society. She was pretty and had especially beautiful brown eyes and hair. At sixteen she had a baby girl out of wedlock and after some time joined one of most prestigious brothels in the city."

"While there she had the affair with the young prince of Wales and he, fortunately for her, wrote numerous letters expressing his love and in much detail the why of that love. Later she had a short marriage to a man twice her age, divorced, and then a second marriage that had her married to Ali Kamel Fahmy Bey and taken off to Egypt to become the bride of a dominant Muslim. He insisted she convert to Islam and dress and behave in accordance to that religion. When faced with life under those conditions she made the decision to end that marriage in the most direct way possible. She convinced Ali Kamel to take her to London to see the newest opera of the time, The Merry Widow. Murdering your husband in Egypt would, by law, led to an immediate execution but in London there would be at least the opportunity of a trial."

"At 2:30 in the morning on July 10, 1923, after attending the opera and in their hotel room at the Savoy, she shot him multiple times in the back and in the head. Armed with the plea of abuse and infidelity, and a box of very detailed letters from the next in line to be King of England, the judge ruled in her favor. She lived out the rest of her life in comfort in an apartment opposite the Ritz Hotel in Paris until her death at age 80 in 1971."

Suz, exhaling an noisy end of story breath, snuggled in closer to Walt, wished him pleasant dreams and that it was time for them to get some sleep. A knocking on their door three hours later wakened them and Walt staggered over to it, dressed only in his briefs, to find Albert, with Loretta using her walker, hidden behind him.

# Chapter 50

"Walt, we need a favor. There's a hundred people out front. Reporters, TV crews and cameras everywhere. It's awful. I am afraid to open my own front door."Albert had a panicked look and was having a hard time formulating the the words to say this. Loretta was hanging onto Albert's shirt with one hand while supporting herself with her walker, holding onto it tightly with the other.

Walt gave them a reassuring smile and said that he and Suz would take of things and that they should go back to their bedroom. "Give us thirty minutes outside and I think we can get them all to leave. Leaving satisfied and maybe even able to make the evening local news."

Ten minutes later Walt and Suz were dressed in their western outfits, both looking exceptionally good. They made their entrance onto the porch and the murmur that went through the crowd out in front of the house was in appreciation of the unexpected and photogenic couple that had come out to greet them.

Walt quickly introduced himself as Walter Wainwright and Suz as his fiance, Suzanne Sussman. That he would try to give them the information they needed to understand what had taken place here late last night and as this was a nice, quiet neighborhood he asked that when he finished that they would leave without any shouted questions or other disturbances.

"Albert Morgan and his wife, Loretta, have lived in this house for over fifty years, watched their son go through the school system here and then head off to UCLA for college. This is their home and downstairs is Albert's gemology laboratory. This is their space and I am asking all of you to respect it."

Walt paused and he could sense he had started with the right tenor and then continued, "Suzanne and I became involved with some missing jewelry searches by one of those chance happenings that occur occasionally. We had stopped for a few days in Dubois, Wyoming and met an older, lifetime resident. She lived in town in a small house and on one wall she had a collage of photos featuring the silent film star Mabel Normand. In college Suzanne had done a project on Charlie Chaplin and she recognized him and several others in the photographs. This led to the conversation about how her mother and father had worked for Mabel Normand for fifteen years during the early days of silent films."

Again Walt paused, then made the connection to the jewelry that had them in Beverly Hills. "The woman with the photo collection had been adopted by her parents as a baby born to a close friend of Mabel Normand who had died shortly after giving birth. Mabel gave her parents a diamond necklace to help them financially in raising the little girl. The necklace had been given to her by an Egyptian prince, Mohammad Ali Ibrahim, who had romanced her at one time. They could sell the individual diamonds as necessary and the almost empty necklace was shown to us on one of our visits."

"Suzanne and I are researchers, curious on almost any subject, and within a few hours we had determined we might have found the missing Tiffany's Hazelnut necklace. It had first been introduced at the 1889 Paris Exposition with a pendant that later had seemed to have also disappeared. Two of the diamonds from Dubois had been sold to a young gemologist here in Beverly Hills, California. Suzanne made contact with that gemologist and we are now standing on his front porch. For your information a photograph of the Hazelnut necklace and pendant is shown on page 69 in the book Tiffany Diamonds. We then started looking for the missing pendant."

Walt took break and then made the next connection for the entranced audience. "Prince Ibrahim, the twenty year old playboy out chasing the young starlets, was a second cousin twice removed, or something like that, from King Fuad of Egypt who's wife, the Queen at the time, was Nazli Sabri. It was from her jewelry box that the young prince had taken the Hazelnut necklace and pendant. It appears that Miss Normand liked and kept the necklace, but not the pendant. We think the pendant was returned to the Queen's jewelry box and later was in it when Nazli came to Los Angeles in 1946. It would end up in Albert Morgan's possession when Nazli wanted to have it modified."

"You will have to do some research to put the pieces together but the real story is about Queen Nazli and her youngest daughter, Fathia, that is pertinent to what occurred here last night. The important date is December 10, 1976 and it is the lost Queen Nazli tiara of the necklace and tiara set made for her by Van Cleef and Arpels that is important. The necklace alone was auctioned in 2015 by Sotheby and purchased by Van Cleef and Arpels for $4,282,000. This places a value on the tiara to make it's finding of such importance. It was in Albert Morgan's possession since that fateful day in 1976 until very early this morning when it was taken away in a Brinks's armored truck."

"Last night and early this morning the missing tiara was being authenticated, purchased by Sotheby to auction and taken back to New York. It is it being found that is the story. Albert Morgan had hidden it all those years and thought it was now time to bring it back into the public domain. He had also come into the possession of the Hazelnut pendant after Queen Nazli had him convert the major diamond of the pendant into a ring for her to keep and he had kept the remnants."

"The morning of December 10, 1976 Queen Nazli gave the ring to a close friend of Fathia's daughter and that afternoon brought the tiara to Albert Morgan for safe keeping. Nazli had been in bankruptcy for several years by this time and had hidden the ring and the tiara from the court. It is that day, the day she and Fathia were to return to Egypt, that will explain to you what caused what has happened here. It is your job to find that out and explain it to your readers and viewers.."

Walt then said in a polite but forceful way that it was now time for all of them to leave and that with some effort on their own that they could have a good story to tell.

As the last of the crowd was exiting a shrill, female voice cried out, "Oh my god, he killed her. Fathia's ex-husband killed her in his mother's apartment."

# Chapter 51

Suz took Walt's hand and they turned towards the open doorway into the house. As they entered they could clearly hear the plaintive cry announcing the death of Fathia.

Suz hesitated but Walt pulled her toward him and back into the house, shutting the door behind them. "I hope it is over. It ended as I had hoped. The press has the story to tell. Thanks to whoever that was that had just looked up the date and Fathia finding the New York Times headline and crying out the news of the murder. They will now start the research and by this afternoon and evening it will be a headline news story."

Albert coughed loud enough to indicate his presence, and with Loretta next to him both were looking relieved and had smiles on their faces. "That went very well, Walt. You are a good speaker and that was a good speech. I have hope that all this may be over. I need you and Suz to help me decide what to do with the money. We don't need it and I don't want any of it. You two deserve something out of all this but let's get some breakfast first and then let it play out."

It was quiet in the house, almost like a death had occurred. They ate in silence, even the sounds of eating seemed muted. Suz then addressed her own thoughts, "That was an interesting way to start the morning. To see all those people out front and then to listen to Walt speaking to them. Albert, you heard all of it, didn't you?" and not letting him answer she continued, "That was something that I have never seen before. Walt had the press in his hands, told them what they needed to know and where to go to find out the rest that they needed. Then asked them to leave and they did. That was the press out there and they were polite and respectful."

She was looking at Walt as she said this and the realization of what this man she had been with for only five weeks had with words and people she had never suspected. It was first with admiration of his leadership but that was turning into fear of not being sure of where this talent might lead them.

Albert was also watching the two of them and he also was thinking that what had just occurred on his front porch this morning would not be lost on all of those listening to what had been said, and how it was said. One or two of the press that had just witnessed it would recognize the leadership qualities that Walt possessed. He had almost forgotten the fear he had that morning of what was to come after passing on the tiara and seeing all those faces wanting to know about his secrets and promises to an ex-Queen of Egypt.

Loretta changed the subject by suddenly announcing that Robert and Angela would be coming tomorrow and would be staying for a week. She seemed happy at entering the conversation and Albert nodded to her and said it was going to be nice to have them here.

Suz then added that this afternoon at five o'clock it would be exactly five weeks since Walt had rescued her from atop her pile of belongs behind a closed restaurant in

Lander, Wyoming. Tossed out of an ex-friends ex-boy friend's house on Wednesday, September sixth to today, Wednesday October eleventh. She added, "Every day an adventure, every day better than the day before and every day more in love with him." She stood up, excused herself and left for their bedroom.

Albert looked first at Loretta and she nodded to him in the unspoken language of couples that have been together for years that he should tell Walt to go to her. He did and added, "You will never find another like her. Never hesitate telling her that and she needs to know this now. What will happen in the next few days could change your lives. You will need her to help get you through what is about to happen."

Walt did understand this, or at least thought he did, and what did happen that afternoon and evening proved them both to be wrong.

# Chapter 52

Suz was sitting on the edge of the bed looking out the window when Walt came into the room and he went directly to her, sitting down beside her. She turned to look at him and he could see the moisture forming in her eyes. He took her hands in his and pulled her closer.

"We will go through whatever comes our way together. Always together. I can't and won't think it can be any other way. Together. I promise you that. Nothing is more important than being with you the rest of my life," was said by Walt leaving no room for any doubts.

"I needed you to say that. What happened out on the porch this morning made me realize how special you are. What a gift you have when speaking to others, not just to me. Our world desperately needs someone like you to guide it right now and I am afraid others are going to recognize this and come  to take you away from me."

They sat several minutes looking into the landscaped backyard where two squirrels were putting on a display of hide and seek between, and in, two small trees. Speed and acrobatic leaps around and up into the trees had both Walt and Suz watching in the silence until the squirrels finally ran up into the same tree and disappeared into the foliage.

Suz moved to Walt and pulled him down on the bed whispering in his ear, "I can keep up with you. You won't get away from me. If things get too tough we can hide out in some tree branches that only we know about. Is that good enough for you?"

"Yes," was Walt's quick reply.

There was a knock on the door and Loretta, speaking in a clear voice, announced that Albert was putting out some lunch makings on the kitchen table and they could fix what they wanted. Albert and she were going to take a rest for a while. Suz went to the door, opened it to see Loretta with her walker making her way slowly down the hall. She called out a thank you but wasn't sure if she had heard it.

The five o'clock news that evening featured, on most of the local stations, the news of the finding of the Queen Nazli's tiara at a local gemologist home and the story of it having been hidden there since December 10, 1976. The stories then varied but all included the last few years of Nazli's and her daughter Fathia's lives. Several of programs started with the recording of the young women crying out that Fathia's ex-husband had killed her in his mother's apartment.

The cameras had caught the couple on the porch, identified them as Walter Wainwright and Suzanne Sussman, in a very good way that set the stage for Walt's comments. The story was covered accurately and ended with some footage of the press leaving in the orderly way that it had happened.

Even Loretta followed the accounts on the television with interest and commented how good Walt and Suz looked on their front porch. Most of Walt's comments came over clearly with very little editing. It was good news coverage and made for good television.

It was not repeated on the evening news, or even on the late edition. Other than the weather and sports it was all coverage of Gaza, Israel and Hamas. Albert's gemology telephone rang several times but then went silent the rest of the evening. It was welcomed, but disappointing.

That evening there was some additional traffic on the Morgan's street, but not much. No one stopped to knock on the door. Even the neighbors didn't seem to care about what had happened early that morning.

Robert and Angela arrived just before lunch the following day and the group of six had a good visit during the two hours at the table. Robert mentioned the possibility of a golf game but Walt and Suz thought it was time they headed back to Dubois. They left the next morning, Friday the thirteenth, spending one hour in Las Vegas for a restroom stop. Suz had put twenty dollars into a slot machine, won forty in ten minutes, and they walked away satisfied with their visit.

As they had left the traffic of the Los Angeles basin and crested Cajon Pass Walt was sure they were not being tailed and started to relax. Suz knew by the way he was continuously looking in the rear and side view mirrors that he was checking for a tail but was also content when finally seeing him relax.

Not wanting to drive through Salt Lake City after dark they started looking for a place to stay for the night as they approached Spanish Forks, ending up at the Microtel Inn in Springville. Dinner was at the nearby Cracker Barrel. It seemed lonely and unfriendly compared to the excitement and company with Albert and Loretta in Beverly Hills. They wished they had stayed one more night.

Maybe played golf with Robert and Angela instead of heading home.

When the two body guards had left that morning they gave a verbal report to Walt. Other than the two men in the car down the street that had left after the Brinks truck pulled out they had seen nothing suspicious. They had even circulated at the news event and hadn't seen anyone there that didn't belong. Last night had been quiet and again nothing was detected that was out of ordinary.

Overnight at the motel was satisfactory, as was the breakfast, if that was what you were used to having. With a stop for gas, and a short walk around a small park along the way, had them driving into the Dubois Campground at three o'clock. A careful inspection of the van had them inside, looking at each other knowing that the intriguing search for the diamonds, and the people who possessed them, was over.

Suz said it first, "What are we going to do now? Go fishing, play golf, go out to dinner at the Lone Buffalo?"

Walt took her hand and suggested they go down to their favorite bench by the river and ask it's advice. They had no sooner got comfortable with Walt's arm around Suz, holding her tight against him, then his phone chirped an incoming call.

# Chapter 53

"Hey Walt, this is Larry. I am back in D.C. and it looks like I will be here for a while. Are you and Suz still thinking about buying the cabin?" was asked and then answered before Walt could respond, "They have destroyed it. Totally gone. In two days removed everything inside and then set off the charges. Christ, the whole building had charges that took out the back half and created a landslide that covered up the rest, Some splintered boards are left from the veranda and I was told all you can see is what looks like the what is left of an old miner's cabin."

Walt was silent for a moment, then asked, "The place was set up with explosives. All the time I was there it could have been blown up at any time?"

Larry didn't say anything at first and then offered that Walt's encounter with the Los Angeles press was being shown around the office. "You and Suz looked good up there on the porch and you sure had the press under control. Might be another position here if you want it. Press secretary. Biden could sure use some one that could make a little sense on what is going on in the White House right now. Then again, maybe not."

There was another awkward pause, then Larry said his good-bye and the line was broken.

Suz stood up, took Walt's hands and pulled him up. "Let's go back up to the van and hide from the rest of the world. I want to be alone with you. Find something to eat and then crawl under the covers and pretend nothing is happening anywhere that is not right or good. Mister Roberts can sing to us a song about being here in the neighborhood and maybe when we wake up tomorrow things will be better."

The hot oatmeal with raisins and brown sugar tasted good for dinner and even if it was still early Suz's suggestion of hiding under the covers in bed was a good one. This night the comfort of just being together was enough and in the small space of the van the greater space outside could be ignored.

The next morning a walk up towards Ollie's was chosen after breakfast and when they got near they spotted him sitting on his picnic table. A welcome back and how did things go at Albert's was asked and Walt gave Ollie most of the details. The story about the tiara was accepted by Ollie with a good laugh. "Hidden away for fifty years in Albert's safe. Maybe worth six million dollars now. Sotheby taking it away in a Brinks Armored Truck in the middle of the night. I wish I could have been there to see it happen," was said by Ollie with his eyes dancing and the biggest grin either Walt or Suz had ever seen on him.

"I have something to show you two. Not diamonds but something more valuable. At least I think so!" was said by Ollie and he walked them a short way back along the path they had come up for their visit. He stopped by an old surveyors stake that was laying on the ground. Picking it up he placed it to vertical, pushing it down in the soft soil enough to have it stand on it's own.

"This is the corner of my property and another  lot starts here having 200 feet of river frontage. I bought it to build a house for myself next to my parents about the same time your tiara was put in Albert's hands. I never got around to do it. I was comfortable living with my parents and they liked having me be there. As they got older it was even more important and then they passed on. Now I don't want to live anywhere else. I have the drawings I drew up for the house I had planned to build and if I do say so they are pretty damn good ones."

Walt and Suz were looking around where they were standing and realized what a beautiful place it was. An expansive view of the river below and enough big trees to shelter them from the highway. Everything that made the placement of Ollie's home so nice was duplicated here.

Ollie then made the offer in a whisper, "If you will build the house I designed, and place it where I wanted it to be, I will sell you the lot for one dollar. I will give you the plans and the model I built. We can talk about any changes you would like and they can be incorporated if it doesn't change the original too much. I would like to see what it would have been if I had built it all those years ago."

Suz looked at Ollie fondly and asked if she and Walt could spend some time with his dream and see if it could come true for the three of them.

Walt asked Suz if she could nail a stud to the plate. She smiled in a mischievous way and told him that if he would load up her tool belt with eight and sixteen penny nails, give her a good hammer and then get out of her way, she would get the house built. "I bet we could have it closed in by the middle of December."

And it was.

# ABOUT THE AUTHOR

Art Myers was born in 1935 and grew up in the small southern California town of La Mesa. He graduated from San Diego State College in 1958 with a BS Degree in Engineering. Several employments in the Military Industrial Complex lasted until the end of 1969. His first layoff was in 1961 and he spent the fall months working as construction labor in Mammoth Lakes, CA and the winter of 1962 skiing in Aspen, Colorado. Another stint in engineering and a second layoff occurred which found him with a wife, daughter, house payments and just beginning what became a thirty year career as a professional sculptor. Interspersed in that thirty years were a variety of residences and occupations for both he and his wife. Retiring in 2002 they bought a sail boat and spent ten years living aboard and cruising both US Coasts. They have lived in a variety of places including Saratoga, CA, Aspen and Loveland, CO, Lake Forest, IL and currently Vero Beach, FL.

His first book was an autobiography, *My Story, How A Young Boy From California Ended Up An Old Man In Florida*, written for family and friends in 2015. He has now completed seven works of fiction, *Andrew's Piano, Ed Adams Chases A Dream, A New Life For Robert Johnson, 10,000 Years Before Present, Ed Adams Touches The Stars, Cynthia's Dreams* and *Wainwright*.

www.ingramcontent.com/pod-product-compliance
Lightning Source LLC
Chambersburg PA
CBHW070351200726
48294CB00003B/835